OUT OF THE MIST

GOLDEN FILLY SERIES

1. *The Race*

2. *Eagle's Wings*

3. *Go for the Glory*

4. *Kentucky Dreamer*

5. *Call for Courage*

6. *Shadow Over San Mateo*

7. *Out of the Mist*

8. *Second Wind*

9. *Close Call*

10. *Winner's Circle*

OUT OF THE MIST

LAURAINE SNELLING

BETHANY HOUSE PUBLISHERS
MINNEAPOLIS, MINNESOTA 55438

Published by Bethany House Publishers
A Ministry of Bethany Fellowship, Inc.
11300 Hampshire Ave., Minneapolis, Minnesota 55438

Printed in the United States of America

Library of Congress Cataloging-in-Publication Data

Snelling, Lauraine.
    Out of the mist / Lauraine Snelling.
       p. cm. — (Golden filly series ; bk. 7)
    Summary: Despite her gift with horses and her success at having
won the Triple Crown, sixteen-year-old Tricia continues to doubt the
God who has allowed her father to die.

    [1. Horse reacing—Fiction. 2. Death—Fiction. 3. Fathers and
daughters—Fiction. 4. Christian life—Fiction.] I. Title.
II. Series: Snelling, Lauraine. Golden filly series ; bk. 7.
PZ7.S6770u   1993
[Fic]—dc20   93–27122
                                                 CIP
ISBN 1-55661-338-5   AC

To my dad,

Laurel,

who gave me my first horse,

a stubborn Shetland pony named Polly,

and who set me back on when I fell off.

Thanks for loving me,

even through those in-spite-of years.

LAURAINE SNELLING is a full-time writer who has authored a number of books, both fiction and non-fiction, as well as written articles for a wide range of magazines and weekly features for local newspapers. She also teaches writing courses and trains people in speaking skills. She and her husband, Wayne, have two grown children and make their home in California.

Her lifelong love of horses began at age five with a pony named Polly and continued with Silver, Kit, Rowdy, and her daughter's horse Cimeron, which starred in her first children's book *Tragedy on the Toutle*.

CHAPTER ONE

What do you do when you're only sixteen and your father has died? You've reached the pinnacle of success, winning the Triple Crown, about the highest honor in thoroughbred horse racing. Where do you go but down?

Tricia Evanston tried to stop the questions from racing through her mind but she didn't seem to have control over much of anything anymore. What did it all mean? Would she feel like the bottom of a manure pit for the rest of her life?

She rubbed the sand off her feet and drew them up to rest on the red plaid blanket she'd spread on the beach. After clamping her arms around her bent legs, she leaned her chin on her knees and stared out at the horizon. Only here at the beach did she seem to find any peace, any trace of the song.

Trish shifted her gaze to the seagulls wheeling and dipping on the air currents above her. They looked so free. Held up by the air. *Do seagulls cry?* she wondered. She hadn't cried since the day her father died a month ago—until yesterday—and now she couldn't seem to quit.

"Well, do you cry?" she shouted at one bird hovering so close she could see the black ring around his yellow beak. He shrieked back at her and let the wind carry him away. "You just wanted something to eat, you didn't want to talk. I don't want to talk, either. Talking hurts. Crying hurts. Everything hurts."

She reached in her cooler for something to feed him but all she found was an orange. That was one good thing about living in California—the fresh oranges. She dug into the stem end with her thumbnail and pulled back the peel.

The gull returned, tracking her movements with a beady eye. When she tossed up a peeling, he snatched it up but dropped it immediately.

"You're smarter than I thought. I don't eat the peelings either." Trish chewed each juicy section, wiping her chin with the back of a tanned hand. She flipped a section up toward the gull. He dropped that too. "Don't like oranges, period, huh?" When she finished, she glared at her chemistry book and flopped back on the blanket.

Her outstretched hand grazed the journal her father had kept in the months before he died. When she turned her head, the carved wooden eagle she'd given him for their last Christmas together lay right in her line of vision.

Eagle's wings. The song from Isaiah 40 had been her theme song. Only yesterday had she finally heard it again, deep within the hidden places of her mind and heart. She listened intently. Against the thunder of the surf and shriek of the gulls, was it still there? Trickling through and dancing on the sunbeams?

She closed her eyes. *Please, let me hear it again,* her soul pleaded. I need the song. ". . . raise you up on eagle's wings . . ." It was so faint maybe she only imagined the words. ". . . bear you on the breath of God . . ." It flowed from within her now, growing stronger, like a stream rushing downhill. ". . . and hold you in the palm of His hand."

Trish wrapped her hands around her shoulders. If she reached out with only a fingertip she would surely touch the *hand*, it felt so real. She waited, hoping for more of the song, but as it faded away, the peace remained.

When a cloud darkened the sun that slid on its downward trail, she took a deep breath, shivering slightly in the breeze. Could she hold on to this feeling on the way back to San Mateo and through the days ahead? Or was it only here at the beach it came to her?

Carefully, so as not to disturb her fragile feelings, Trish picked up her own just-begun journal along with her father's, wrapped them in a towel along with the eagle, and slipped them into her pack. Then folding the blanket and picking up the *Swingline* cooler, she slogged her way through the soft sand to the base of the eroded sandstone cliff.

The trail staggered its way up through the rocks, now hiding, then pitching vertically. It took sure feet and a gymnastic balance to make it to the parking lot with full hands. Trish stopped at the rim to catch her breath.

She listened. Yes, it was still there. Stowing her gear in the trunk, Trish dusted off her feet and slipped on her sandals. She glanced in the side mirror and despaired of ever getting a brush through her thick, wavy, midnight hair. That's what someone had called it once, the color of midnight. She liked the sound of that. Wearing her hair in a braid down her back was the only way to control it. Trish fluffed her bangs and covered her green eyes with dark glasses. Her nose looked about ready to peel—again. Would she ever learn to use sunscreen?

Trish unlocked the door of her red Chrysler convertible—the car presented her when her colt Spitfire won the Kentucky Derby—and slid behind the wheel. She listened intently. The song—yes, she could hear it.

She drove slowly out the bumpy road, past the towering eucalyptus trees, and turned left onto Highway One. With each sweeping curve up the hill, leaving the town of Half Moon Bay behind, the song grew fainter. By the time she reached the College of San Mateo campus, located high on the hill overlooking San Francisco Bay, her song, like the beach, was only a memory.

Trish had come from her home in Vancouver, Washington, to stay with friends of the family, the Finleys, in hopes that the busyness at the track and a make-up chemistry course at the College of San Mateo would help get her mind off her father's death.

Welcome back to the real world—and a D in chemistry. Tonight was a lab, and that was always more interesting than the lecture—or the quizzes. As she and her partner Kevin lit up the Bunsen burner, Trish studied the experiment instructions.

While he added the first two elements, her mind flipped back to the beach. "And then what?" Kevin's sharp voice brought her back.

"Then heat until the color changes to . . ."

The compound fuzzed, smoked, and smelled atrocious.

"What are you trying to do—kill us both?" Kevin dropped the test tube in a deep sink where it shattered.

"Clear the room, everyone," the teacher's assistant ordered, turning the fans on high.

When Trish finally quit coughing, along with everyone else, lab time was over and she was still further behind. An F sure wouldn't help her grade any.

It was a miracle she was able to reach the condominium with her eyes streaming like they were. She dragged herself up the stairs and, after closing her bedroom door, threw herself across the bed. She buried her face in a pillow to muffle the heart-wrenching sobs. Trying to pray only made her cry harder.

"Trish," Martha Finley, wife of breeder/trainer Adam Finley, and Trish's "other mother," poked her head in the doorway after knocking several times. Without another word, she crossed the room and, sitting down on the bed, gathered the sobbing girl into her arms. She murmured soothing sounds and stroked Trish's hair, allowing her to cry.

"I—I'm so tired—of cry—ing."

"I know. But tears are necessary when you've been wounded like you have. Only by crying and talking through your grief and confused feelings will you ever begin to heal."

"I want my d-a-d."

"I know you do, honey. I know."

When the sobs finally lessened, Martha handed Trish a tissue.

"Everything is such a mess. I can't think straight. I can't concentrate on anything. It's like I live in a big black fog." Trish reached for another tissue and Martha handed her the box.

"I just want to run away—and keep on running."

"But you'll take yourself with you," Martha answered wisely.

"That's the pits."

"Ummm."

Silence but for a hiccup and sniffs.

"Martha, I want my dad back." The tears flowed again. "I *need* my father."

Martha held Trish close, rocking back and forth and crooning the songs that mothers have used through the ages to comfort their children.

When Trish finally crawled between the covers, she felt like a wrung-out stable rag. Swollen-shut eyes, raw, burning nose, and a heart that weighed two tons didn't make her feel any better. While she feared another night of tossing and turning, sleep crept in before she could turn over even once.

The song—that was it. Trish opened her eyes to check the clock. Had the song come before she slept or just now as she awoke? It didn't matter. It had come—and not only at the beach.

She threw the covers back and leaped from the bed. This was sure to be a better day. The song had come. She flew into the bathroom and turned on the shower. As she stepped under the pelting water, she was humming.

———

Fog swirling about the streetlights and blanketing the ground made driving to the track an exercise in concentration. Trish squinted through the windshield, driving slow enough that she could stop before hitting anything—or anyone. Morning sounds at the track seemed muffled by the gray miasma.

She left her car in the parking lot and trotted through the gate, lifting a hand in greeting to the guard. She dodged to the side as a bug boy, the fringe of his leather chaps dangling in the breeze, sped past on his bicycle. A pony-rider on a bay quarterhorse plodded past on his way to escort another high-strung thoroughbred out to the track. Trish knew that watching her feet instead of the traffic around her could cause an injury, so she kept her head upright. This morning that wasn't difficult.

Gatesby tossed his head and whinnied a greeting as
soon as she turned the corner into the Finley stalls. Firefly, in the stall next to him, added her welcome. Trish
kept a careful eye on the gelding, she didn't feel like
getting nipped today—or any day for that matter.
Gatesby harbored the genes of a natural rowdy, not ma-
licious, but a bite in fun hurt just as much as one in
anger.

Trish scratched behind his ears, always keeping one
hand on his halter. "You old goof-off. Been buggin' anyone yet today?"

"*Sí, el estúpido caballo me mordió,*" Juan, one of the
grooms, told her. He pointed to a spot on his arm, shaking his head.

Firefly nickered again.

"Your turn, I know." Trish left the gelding and ducked
her shoulder under the filly's chin. Standing like this, his
head draped over Trish's shoulder, was Spitfire's favorite
position. Trish swallowed a lump at the thought of her
big black colt, now a stud at BlueMist Farms in Kentucky. Oh, how she missed him! But when a colt has won
the Triple Crown, he goes into syndication and retires to
stud. The money from that transaction would keep her
family comfortable for years to come.

But that knowledge didn't make things easier for
Trish. She gritted her teeth and, giving the filly one last
scratch, moved on to the next stall.

Adam Finley and Carlos Montanya, the head groom,
stood inside discussing the problems the colt was having
as they wrapped his legs for the morning work.

"Who'm I doing first?" Trish asked after waiting for
a pause in the conversation.

Adam turned, a smile creasing his apple cheeks.

"Morning, Trish. Think we'll go with Diego's. Juan is saddling him now." Finley unhooked the canvas gate across the stall door and stepped outside. "How you doin' this morning?" He peered into her face and nodded. "Better, I can tell."

"Martha blabbed."

He nodded again. "Yes, and we're grateful."

"For what?"

"You." He reached inside the tack room/office and brought out her whip. "Be careful out there this morning. Everyone's kinda antsy."

How could such a simple comment, that the Finleys were grateful for her, make Trish want to bawl, she wondered. She raised her knee for the mount.

Two horses later, Adam's advice paid off. A horse galloping beside her spooked at something and leaped sideways, crashing into her mount's shoulder. Her horse stumbled badly and within a few paces, pulled up limping. Trish dismounted and led him back to the barn.

"If I'd just paid closer attention," she grumbled to Adam when she reached the row of stalls.

"Lass, for crying out loud, you can't foresee everything. You kept him from a bad fall. Coulda done a lot more damage, and hurt yourself on top of it." He stripped the saddle off so the stable hands could wash the animal down and pack the injured leg in ice.

But the near-accident ruined the morning for Trish, knocking her right back into her pit of despair.

A black horse galloping by reminded her of Spitfire— the way he held his head, the way he begged for a run, his deep grunts when he ran hard. It seemed like months since she'd seen her horse. Would he still remember her?

Thoughts of Spitfire brought thoughts of home. How

were the babies, Miss Tee and Double Diamond, coming along? How she needed a hug from her mother, and a good old bad time from her brother, David. She watched out for the other working horses and paid attention to her own mount, but one part of her mind visited Runnin' On Farm—and home. When could she go back?

I'll call as soon as I'm done with these beasts, she promised herself.

The rising sun had burned off all but stray wisps of the morning fog, which hid in the lowest places by the time the last horse was worked according to Adam's schedule.

"You got any mounts this afternoon?" Adam asked when Trish had dropped down into a faded-green director's chair. When she shook her head, he said, "Good. I'm taking you out for lunch." When she started to object, he raised a hand. "No, I know you have homework, and you'd probably rather head for the beach, but we need to talk." He looked up as Carlos stuck his head in the door with a question. After giving the needed answer, Adam turned back to Trish. "Someplace without so many interruptions." He grinned at her. "Besides, it's still overcast at the beach and will stay so all day."

Trish glanced at her watch. "Can I go home and change first?"

"If you want. I'll meet you at the Peking Gardens at noon."

When Trish entered her bedroom, the first thing she did was dial home. The phone rang and rang. "You'd think they'd have the answering machine on at least," she muttered as she dropped the receiver back in the cradle.

She tried her best friend, Rhonda. At least they had the answering machine on.

When she looked in the bathroom mirror, she saw that tiny spatters of mud had given her freckles. She washed them away and scrubbed her hands. The face in the mirror didn't smile back. A smile was too much effort.

She shucked off her clothes and tossed them into the hamper. Damp mornings messed up her jeans. Maybe she should wear chaps like some of the others. She looked in the mirror again. *Maybe I should just quit.*

The thought scared her. It was coming too frequently lately.

"All you need is one good win," she pointed her hairbrush at the grim face.

And that's about as likely as you acing a chem test, her little nagging voice rejoined. *You know, if you'd . . .*

Trish slammed the hairbrush down on the counter and left the room. All she needed was one more person telling her what to do, even if it was her own head.

Adam waited for her in a corner booth. While the restaurant had many patrons, the tables around them were empty for the moment. Trish slid into the red vinyl booth seat across from him. An icy Diet Coke stood in front of her.

"Thanks." She sipped, and set the glass back down. A sigh escaped from deep within.

Adam reached across the table and covered her clenched hands with his own. "How can I help you, Tee?"

Tee, her father's pet name for her, did it. Trish covered her brimming eyes with her hands.

Would she ever stop crying?

CHAPTER TWO

"Oh, lass, I'm so glad for you."

Trish heard the words, but they didn't make any sense. Here she couldn't seem to quit crying, and Adam said he was glad for her! Her thoughts tumbled over each other, shutting off the tears like a faucet.

She mopped her eyes with the napkin in front of her, then dug in her purse for a tissue. After blowing her nose and wiping her eyes again, she took a deep breath and blew it out. She stared at the face across from her.

"How come you and Martha both say you're happy to see me crying? Seems kinda mean to me." Trish sniffed, and sipped her Diet Coke.

"Well, Trish, these weeks since your father died, you've been all frozen up inside. And that's not healthy." He shook his head. "Not at all."

Without looking up, Trish said, "It didn't hurt as bad that way. Now I hurt all the time."

"Maybe, but the healing has begun. You have to let the feelings out, cry them out, express them, in order to deal with all that has happened."

"But my dad is still gone."

"I know. And nothing can bring him back. But you *will* be able to go on, and one day you'll look around you

17

and life will be good again. Not the *same*, but good again."

Trish let the tears spill over and stream down her cheeks. When she could speak, she took courage and brought up the question that was scaring her: "Do you think I'll be any good as a jockey again?"

"Oh yes. You have been given a wondrous gift with horses, and that hasn't been taken from you. It may be put under wraps for a while, but it will come back."

"You really think so?"

"I don't just think, I *believe* so."

———

Trish kept his words in her mind as she drove back to the Finleys' condominium. The sun, now hot on her back as she climbed the stairs to the front door, begged her to come out and enjoy it. Once in her room, she changed into a lime green swimsuit and, picking up her homework, went out on the deck off her room for some serious studying. The words and symbols danced on the page in the bright sunlight, so she went back inside for her sunglasses.

Within a few minutes, she went back inside and down to the kitchen for a glass of ice tea. Next she needed a highlighter. By the time she finally got settled and tried to concentrate, the words swam before her eyes. She rolled over to her stomach and squinted against the glare. Within moments she lay fast asleep.

That evening Trish walked in the door of her chemistry class, homework unfinished, and suffering a headache that made her sick to her stomach. And if she had touched water to her skin, it would have sizzled. She sat straight up in the chair, without touching the back of the seat. Her clothing was painful enough.

How could you have done such a stupid thing? Nagger perched on her right shoulder, she was sure. *To fall asleep in the hot afternoon sun like that, when you've hardly been in the sun at all . . .*

Trish just groaned and rested her head in her hand.

The teacher walked to the front of the room and announced a quiz, worth ten points.

Trish covered her eyes with her hand and shuddered. She answered only two of the ten questions, got up and left. There was no point in staying. She could hardly spell her own name, let alone pay attention to a lecture she didn't understand in the best of times.

All the way home, she could think only of the beach. At least at the beach she felt closer to her father. And out there she could think; she could hear her song. *Tomorrow,* she promised herself. *As soon as you're done at the track tomorrow, you can go to the beach.* She flinched at the sting of her back. Tomorrow she'd keep a shirt on.

She hardly slept that night. Twice she got up and into the shower to cool the burning.

At three A.M. Martha knocked on the door, just after Trish had crawled back into bed. "Trish, what's wrong? Can I come in?"

"Sure. It's just my sunburn. I fell asleep on the deck this afternoon."

"Here, let me see."

Trish pulled up the back of her nightshirt.

"Oh, you poor dear." Martha gingerly touched one spot. "Hang on, I'll be right back." She returned in a few moments, carrying a bottle of green gel. "This will do the trick. Aloe vera, God's burn ointment. Only instead of just using pieces of the plant like we used to, you can

buy it in a bottle now." She sat down on the bed by Trish
and poured some into her hands. "Now, this will feel
cool."

Trish flinched when the stuff touched her back, but
soon breathed a sigh of relief as the cooling strokes took
away the pain.

"Now I think you'll sleep, my dear." Martha stood up
and set the plastic bottle on the nightstand. "Put this on
again when you wake up, and before you leave for the
track, I'll cover your entire back with it."

"Thank you," Trish mumbled, already half asleep.

———

Gatesby was in rare form when Trish took him out
on the track in the morning. He tossed his head and
jigged sideways down the track. "Knock it off, you dun-
derhead." Trish tightened the reins as she scolded him.
Gatesby half reared, ears flat against his head. Trish felt
like clobbering him one, right between those flat ears.
Instead, she pulled him to a stop and waited until he
blew out a deep breath and settled his weight evenly on
all four legs. When his ears pricked forward, she loos-
ened the reins. "All right now, let's see if we can behave."
Gatesby shook his head and set off at a smart walk as if
he'd never acted up in his life.

By the time works were finished, Trish's sunburn
cried for the soothing green gel. She trotted over to the
women's rest room and pulled off her shirt.

"Whoa, that's a bad one." Another jockey turned to
study Trish's flaming back. "Here, let me help you." She
took the bottle and applied the gel.

"Thanks. It feels so much better when someone else
puts it on."

"What'd you do? Fall asleep in the sun?"

Trish nodded. "Dumb, huh?"

"Yeah, well, we've all done it." She leaned closer to the mirror to study a spot on her chin. "You're Trish Evanston, aren't you?" Trish nodded. "You've won the biggies. We were all so excited when a woman won the Triple Crown. We were yellin' and screamin'. The guys thought we were crazy. That colt of yours, he's something else."

"Thanks." Trish leaned a hip against the counter. "What's your name?"

"Oh, sorry, I'm Mandy Smithson." She turned from the mirror. "I want you to know we all feel terrible about your dad." She shook her head. "Tough break."

Trish sniffed and blinked her eyes. "Thanks."

Mandy turned to face her. "Trish, I know how you feel. My mom died from cancer when I was thirteen. She'd been sick for a long time."

"Oh, no. How awful for you."

"Yeah, it was. I never had much of a childhood. And then I kinda went off the deep end. Took me a long time to get back on track, so don't let that happen to you." She touched a finger to Trish's cheek where a tear had fallen. "Don't try to tough it out. I did, and it's not worth it."

"But I can't even ride decent anymore."

"You will. Just takes time, that's all." Mandy squeezed Trish's arm. "Hey, something else I learned. People don't know what to say to you so they look the other way. Makes you feel kinda like you're invisible."

Trish nodded again. "Uh-huh."

"So you smile first. Don't wait for them." She waved with one hand as she left the room. "See ya."

Trish blew her nose with paper from one of the stalls. After taking a deep breath, she left the room. *Invisible*, that's exactly what she felt like sometimes.

After a light lunch, Trish grabbed her bag and walked around the track to the jockey rooms just south of the grandstands. The white building gleamed in the sunlight. Tall palm trees rustled in the breeze in the front courtyard of Bay Meadows Track, where busloads of retired spectators were already disembarking. It promised to be another perfect California day at the track, now that the fog had burned off.

Trish sighed. In spite of the weather, she hadn't had a perfect day here since she arrived. Today she had one mount and that was only because Adam still had faith in her. No one else seemed to want to hire her anymore. Well, after this race she would head for the beach. At least there she felt like there was *some* hope.

She couldn't keep her eyes open even though she sat in the most uncomfortable chair in the room. The conversation of the other women jockeys flowed around her while she tried to study. She scrunched farther down in the chair, flinched from her sunburn, got up, splashed water on her face—and still nodded off.

When someone touched her shoulder, she jerked awake.

"Time to suit up," the attendant said.

Trish checked her watch against the clock on the wall. "Thanks," she mumbled, still caught in the slog of sleep. At least she'd shined her boots and goggles earlier. She pulled on a white sleeveless turtleneck, then her white pants and laced up the front closure. Boots next, and after grabbing her helmet, she made it to the silks keeper and then the scale, the last in line.

"I was beginning to wonder about you," Adam said with a smile when she met him at the stall in the saddling paddock under the grandstands. The layout of the paddock felt so much like the one at Portland Meadows, Trish caught herself looking over her shoulder for David.

At the "rider's up" call, she stroked the filly's nose and ducked under the horse's neck to be tossed into the saddle.

"Now let her get her stride good and keep her off the pace about fourth or so. The track's good and fast and you've only six furlongs, so you need to make your move as you come out of the turn. Remember, this is only her third time out and she's not always quite sure what to do."

Trish nodded in all the right places. She swallowed hard to get her butterflies back down where they belonged. They seemed to be engaged in a somersault contest, at her expense.

"You okay now?" Adam looked up at her before backing the horse out of the stall.

Trish nodded and swallowed again. Down butterflies, down!

The filly pricked her ears at the roar of the crowd as the field of ten trotted out on the track. When they lined up, waiting for the handlers to take each horse into its stall, the entry on their left reared and slashed out at the pony rider. Three men grabbed the animal and wrestled him under control before leading him into position four.

Trish walked her filly into their stall, crooning her song of comfort all the while.

The horse on their right walked in, and two more when number four reared again. The jockey scrambled off this time in case the animal went over backwards.

Again the handlers took the time to work the horse back into the stall and get the jockey remounted.

Trish felt the tension ripple up her back. The filly stamped her front feet and switched her tail. Trish stroked the dark brown neck where dots of moisture revealed the filly's agitation. "Easy, girl. Take it easy."

Silence. A brief, heart-thumping moment and the gates clanged open. They were off.

Number four broke, stumbled, and crashed into the filly as she barely cleared the gate. Trish fought to keep her horse on her feet, and miraculously they made it through. By the time they were running true, the field clustered in front of them and all Trish could see was a solid wall of moving rumps. She started to swing out around when a hole opened in front of her.

She drove the filly in and through the hole to be caught in a box. They were halfway through the turn before she could see another hole, and when they went for it, the filly gave her all. She dove through and headed for the three leaders two lengths in front.

Trish rode her hard, but at the half-mile pole the jockeys went to their whips and number two took off. Trish's filly passed the number three horse and crept up, nose to tail, nose to shoulder, nose to nose, straining for all she had. When the front runner passed the post, Trish and her filly were number two by only a whisker. It took the camera to declare the winner, but Trish knew it before the numbers flashed on the board.

"Good race, lass," Adam commented as he trotted out on the track to snap on a lead line.

"She shoulda had it. What a sweetheart to come back after a bum start like that. They shoulda scratched that stupid beast beside us. And then to let her get caught in a box like I did. Adam, I'm sorry."

"Trish, I said you did a good job." Adam clipped each word, enunciating clearly, as if she were hard of hearing.

Trish shook her head. "She should have won that. A good jockey woulda brought her in to win."

Adam let her rant on. At his "don't be so hard on yourself," Trish just shook her head and, clamping her hands under her saddle, strode over to the scale.

At least now she could go to the beach.

———

She tossed her bag in the backseat and pushed the button to put the top down. Maybe the wind in her hair would blow away the cobwebs. "And maybe all it'll do is make your hair a rat's nest," she grumbled to the face in her mirror as she set her black plastic sunglasses in place.

A gray fog bank hovered just on the horizon, sending high spindrift clouds to tease the sun. The ride was quick and effortless, and Trish could feel herself unwind as she arrived at her favorite spot. An offshore breeze kicked up sand as she tried to lay out her blanket that billowed and flipped up at the corners. Once on the ground, she plunked her cooler in one corner, her schoolbag in another, and herself on the rest.

At least today she wouldn't be tempted to sunbathe and fall asleep. She pulled an orange out of the cooler and, after peeling it, ate the whole thing, ignoring the cries of the gull wheeling above her.

She dug her journal out of her bag and turned to the first blank page. She didn't have too many pages to turn, because writing in a journal like her father had done still wasn't a habit. She bit the end of her pen.

But once she began, the words seemed to flow out of a deep well of despair: *I feel like I'm being jerked around like a yo-yo. Yeah, and by a kid who doesn't know how to use the thing. One minute I'm rolling high and feeling like maybe I'll make it, and the next I'm bouncing on the floor and my string is all wrapped in knots around me.*

Everyone keeps telling me things will be better in time, but how much time? I miss you, Dad, I can't even begin to tell you how much. Why did you leave me? What kind of God takes a father from his kids? Why didn't you quit smoking years ago when we first asked you to?

Trish gritted her teeth. She could feel the anger again, red hot and fiery, flaming in her stomach. The "why's" fueled it higher. She flung herself down on the blanket and clenched her arms around her middle. When she finally rolled over on her back, she winced in pain.

"Ahhh." She sat up and tried to arch her back away from her clothes. She tore into her bag. No green bottle. It was up in the car in her track bag. The pain eased when she turned her back to the breeze, but now her hair blew in her eyes.

She picked up the pen again but the urge to write had flown away like the gull who'd screamed for her orange. She snorted. Yeah, even the gulls yelled at her. She swiped at her eyes again. Whatever happened to that iron will she had?

She couldn't lie on her back because it hurt. She couldn't lie on her stomach because, when the sun did come out, the heat hurt her back. She rolled on her side and pillowed her head on her book bag. At least her chemistry book was good for something!

She lay in that no-man's-land between waking and sleeping until the breeze blew more cold than cool.

Struggling up the cliff helped wake her up, but when raindrops misted the windshield she put the top up.

The foggy mist hovered over the campus too when she arrived, so she pulled on her sweats and, because she was late, ended up in the back row. Keeping awake in class was hard in the best of times, and now certainly wasn't one of those times. She left for home at the break.

"Your mom called," Martha announced when Trish pushed open the door and stumbled in. "Said she'd gotten your message and was sorry the machine was off earlier. Was just a few minutes ago." She glanced up at the clock. "You're home early."

"I just couldn't stay awake. Tomorrow night I meet with my tutor. Maybe he can work a miracle." Trish went to the kitchen and poured herself a glass of ice water. "Good-night."

Once in her own room, Trish dialed the phone and waited for an answer. At the same time, she kicked off her shoes and sweats. "Hi, Mom . . ." Trish got no further. At her mother's "hi," she lost it.

"Oh, Trish, I'm so glad you called." Her mother's words were separated by sniffs. When they'd both calmed down again, Trish could hear her mother's gentle words. "You're finally crying, Trish. Thank you, God, thank you."

Trish blew her nose and wiped her eyes. "Mom, I want to come home." She sniffled again and rolled her eyes toward the ceiling to control the tears. Sometimes the trick worked. She drew in a raggedy breath. "What's happening up there? How's Miss Tee?" The questions poured out.

Trish lay on the bed, feeling limp like the seaweed on the beach.

"David has some really great news," her mother was saying. "Here, I'll let him tell you."

"Hi, baby sister. How ya doing?"

"Not so good."

"I can tell."

"Well, how'd you like to have red, swollen eyes all the time? And the puffier my eyes are, the easier it is to fall asleep. That's the only thing I do well right now."

"How's the chemistry?"

"Don't ask." She grabbed another tissue and blew again. "So what's your news?"

"I've been accepted at the University of Arizona, pre-veterinarian medicine. I'll be leaving the last week in August."

"Oh, David, n-o-o!"

CHAPTER THREE

"Come on, Trish. I'm not going to the ends of the earth. This won't be any different than when I went to Washington State."

"Yes, it will. You'll be farther away." Trish scrubbed her fingers through her hair.

"Not really. Now it'll be air time instead of drive time, so really I'll be closer."

Trish could tell her brother was forcing patience into his voice. Why couldn't she be happy for him? He was finally getting to do what he wanted to after taking a year off college to help at home.

"Hey, look who's been gone the last months."

"I know, David." Trish leaned against the pillows she'd stacked up behind her on the bed. "I guess . . ." She struggled to find the right words. ". . . I guess I don't want any more change. So much has happened that sometimes I'm afraid my whole world is going to explode and fly away in a million pieces—and that I'll never be able to put it all back together again."

"Things will never be the same again, Tee. You can't expect that, and you've got to face it."

"I know."

A silence lengthened between them, but it was comforting, not awkward.

"So, how's your chemistry coming?"

"I *said*, don't ask. Oh, David, how come I'm so stupid when it comes to chemistry? I study and think I have stuff memorized, and when I take the test my brain flies right out the window. The other day I nearly caused everyone to die of smoke inhalation."

"What happened?"

"I was reading the instructions for the experiment to my partner, and I accidentally gave part of the next one. The two didn't mix very well."

David swallowed a chuckle. "You have to pay close attention in the lab."

"Tell me about it. That's the problem, my attention span. It goes to sleep on me every chance it gets." She wiped her nose with a soggy tissue. "And takes my brain and body right along with it. I feel as if I could sleep for years."

"Sounds like you're depressed to me."

"Thank you, Doctor Evanston."

"No, I read some stuff on grieving that Mom gave me. It said depression happens a lot, and wanting to sleep all the time can be part of it."

"Mmmm." Trish pulled on her earlobe. When it hurt, she removed the gold post and laid it on the nightstand. "I gotta hit the books again, David."

"Hey, if you don't make it home before I leave, I'll stop by there on my way. You can show me this beach you keep running away to."

"Sure, sounds good. Good-night, David. Say good-night to Mom. And tell Rhonda and Brad I could use some mail. Or a phone call." She hung up. She was glad she'd called but she didn't feel as good as she'd expected. She picked up her book bag, and the chemistry book fell out on her chest. She felt like throwing it across the room, but managed to calmly open it to the assignment.

She fell asleep at some point and awoke with a terrible thirst. She stared groggily at the clock. *One-thirty.* She staggered to the bathroom, drank some water, and shed her clothes on the way back to her bed. When the alarm rang, Trish felt like pulling the covers over her head and pretending the world didn't exist. Instead, she slammed her fist on the snooze button and drifted off again.

The crowd screamed as she and Spitfire surged across the finish line, winning by two lengths. They did it; they won! She could hear his breathing, whistling like a freight train, his heart pounding against his ribs. The crowd screamed again as they trotted back to the winner's circle.

It wasn't the crowd screaming. Trish reached over and turned off the alarm. She rolled onto her back and closed her eyes again. At least in her dreams she was still a winner. And winning felt so good.

She pushed herself to a sitting position. Maybe she was jinxed without Spitfire! She shook her head. That was crazy. It wasn't as if the only time she won was when she was riding the big black colt, her best friend in all the world. But now Spitfire lived at BlueMist Farms in Kentucky and wasn't even hers any longer. At least not all hers.

She tugged on her clothes, and headed for the track. That was part of the problem, wasn't it? She was so alone. Except for Mandy, the jockey she'd talked to maybe once, the only people she really talked to here were the Finleys and her tutor, Richard. And all he wanted to talk about was chemistry. Yuk!

You just have to make the effort. She wished Nagger

had stayed at home in bed, asleep for about an eternity or so. *Besides, who'd want to be your friend, you're about as much fun as . . . as a chemistry quiz.* Trish slammed the door of her car and the one on her mind also. She did *not* need his advice right now, especially when all it did was make her feel worse. Even if he was right.

At least the horses were glad to see her. Even Gatesby seemed to want some extra loving. Trish scratched ears and cheeks down the line, inhaling the good, honest smell of horse. Even though she wasn't winning, this part of her world seemed right. The horses didn't care if she felt brain dead half the time. Firefly lipped a tendril of hair that framed Trish's face, just like Spitfire used to do, and whuffled in her face.

Trish wrapped her arms around the bright sorrel neck and tried to picture Spitfire there instead. But he wouldn't come in. Was she even losing his memory?

The fogless morning felt good for a change as she worked the string of horses. She would walk some, breeze Firefly, and slow gallop others, all the time following the conditioning program Adam had designed for the horses in his care.

"How'd she do?" Adam asked of a new mare that he'd started training.

"Kinda sluggish. Not what you'd think after all the time she's had off. I don't think she feels tip-top."

Adam nodded. "We'll check her temp. No limping on that right front?"

Trish shook her head. "Gracias," she said as Carlos gave her a leg up on Gatesby, her last mount for the morning. When the gelding didn't act up, she looked at Carlos with a question. He shrugged and shook his head, keeping a wary eye on the horse just the same.

"Okay, what's happening?" she asked after a rather dispirited trot around the oval track. She leaned forward and stroked the dark neck flecked with sweat. "You shouldn't have worked up a sweat. It's back to the barn with you, fella."

"We better check temps all around," Adam said to Carlos when Trish told him what she'd observed.

Trish held the horses' heads while Carlos and Adam checked temperatures. They drew blood on the mare, ready to send it out for diagnosis, when they saw the mare was running a fever.

"What could it be?" Trish asked when the third animal in a row showed a rise in body heat. She walked beside Adam back to the office.

"Who knows?" Adam dropped into his swivel chair and picked up the phone. He pushed the speed dial for the vet. "I think we've got trouble," he said after the greeting. "Anyone else running temps?" He rubbed the back of his neck with one hand. "Okay, see you in a couple of minutes."

"What did he say? Anyone else got trouble?" Trish dropped down to the lid on a green tack box.

Adam shook his head. "Not that he knows of. Carlos, disinfect all the buckets."

"Already doing that. No one was off their feed this morning. But now that mare has a runny nose." Carlos removed his hat to scratch his head.

"Well, she was clean when she came in here." Adam pulled out the record book. "Doc wouldn't have let anything by, and his inspection was only two days ago. She came in at night, right?"

Trish listened to the discussion with one ear while her memory flipped back to the siege of infection they'd had at Runnin' On Farm the fall before. The first time her father'd been in the hospital. She'd had some mighty sick horses. Her stomach turned queasy at the thought. Could *she* have brought back the virus from some other farm she rode for?

The pickup containing the portable veterinarian clinic pulled up at the barn, and the vet climbed out. "Well, let's see what's going on." He raised the door on the rear of the canopy and removed a stainless steel bucket with equipment in it.

Trish watched from the doorway as he checked over the bay mare. She looked droopy all right, and had a runny nose.

"Looks like we better vaccinate the entire string. I'll take that blood sample in, but I'm sure it's going to show herpes virus 1. You know the game plan, and I know you've vaccinated your horses regularly. Where'd this one come from?"

As the discussion continued, Trish stroked the mare's neck and rubbed her ears. "Poor old girl, sorry you caught this. But you keep the bug to yourself, you hear?"

"This should blow over in a week or so, but make sure she drinks plenty of water. If you hear any railes [rattling] in her lungs or the coughing gets really bad, she could develop pneumonia. Keep me posted."

Trish followed him to the truck. "Ah—can I ask you a question?"

"Sure, shoot away." He slung the bucket back in the truck.

"Could I—ah—do you think I brought the virus back from another barn?"

"Naa, she was probably a latent carrier. Wouldn't be surprised if she had it a long time ago and all the stress

of shipping and a new environment brought it on. You
know Adam is really careful about his horses, but not
everyone is as cautious as he is."

"Thanks." Trish felt like someone had just lifted a
load from her shoulders and her stomach settled back
down.

You're beginning to think everything is your fault, Nagger whispered in her ear. *That's not smart, you know.*

Later, as she walked up to the jockey room, Trish
thought ahead to the afternoon program. For a change
her agent had gotten her mounts for two other trainers.
Neither were top horses, but that certainly wasn't sur-
prising. If she could just get them to run.

By the time the third race was called, her resident
troupe of butterflies flipped around on their warm-ups.
She listened to the trainer's instructions carefully. The
gelding did not like being boxed in, and they were in
gate two.

Why didn't they put blinkers on him, Trish thought
as they trotted past the stands. Then tight quarters
wouldn't bother him so much.

"Ya gotta break fast," she told the twitching ears as
the horse shifted from side to side in the gate. "Easy now,
you know what's happening." The singsong was as much
for her as the restless horse under her. "Come on, fella,
I need this win even more than you do."

The gate, the horse, and Trish all exploded at the
same instant. But it was like time stood still for just a
fraction before the gelding caught the first stride. The
first three animals surged stride for stride, but that
pause gave number four the opportunity he needed. Going into the first turn he pounded directly in front of
Trish.

Her mount shook his head, watching the horses on

either side of him more than concentrating on the job he was set to do. Trish swung her whip back once and he leaped forward. But it was a fight all the way to the pole. And they were caught in the middle the entire distance, giving them a fourth.

The trainer looked at her with a blank face. *I told you so*, seemed to hover all around them. All he said was "tough break."

Tough break, my eye, Trish scolded herself all the way back to the jockey room.

And the next race wasn't any better. This time she had the horse in front, just like the trainer told her to do, but he quit running with four lengths to go. They took a show.

"I'm sorry," she told the trainer. "He just quit."

"Yeah, well, that was his first time at a mile. Thought you had it there, though."

"Me, too." As she walked back to the jockey's room, she felt the loneliness return. If only she had someone to talk to. She checked her watch. Rhonda ought to be home now. She headed for the phone and dialed her friend's number.

Trish felt her heart leap when the familiar voice answered on the second ring.

"Hi," Trish cleared her throat, "it's me."

"Trish, I can't believe it. How are you? What's going on? David says you're not doing so well at the track. And how's the beach? You all tanned?"

Trish laughed at the rapid-fire stream of questions. Yup, this was Rhonda all right. Words running over each other. "How can I answer all that at the same time?"

"You can't. I'll make it easy. You won any races lately?"

"Thanks, friend. Get me right where it hurts. I haven't won since Belmont, so that answers another question. I'm not doing well, anywhere, anytime."

"Why don't you come home?"

"Why don't you come down here? We could go school shopping like we never dreamed."

"Oh, I can't. I've got jumping shows coming up the next two weekends. How about after that?"

Trish sighed. "That's so far away. I was hoping you could come now." She leaned against the wall, the phone clamped between her ear and shoulder.

"Sorry, Tee."

"I know. I'll call the travel agent and she'll send you the ticket."

"Hey, you heard from the sexiest jockey in the world?"

"Rhonda!"

"Well, Red Holleran is a hunk in my book."

"He is nice."

"Nice! Nice! Your dog is nice. A hot fudge sundae is yummy. Red is . . ."

"Rhonda, you nut." Trish giggled.

" . . . sweet, likes you a whole lot, rides like a dream, and kisses like a . . ."

"That's enough." Trish strangled on her laughter. "You didn't kiss him."

"No, but you did, and when you just so happened to mention it to your best friend in all the world, your eyes glazed over. That should tell you something."

"Spitfire's my best friend in all the world."

"Okay, your best *human* friend, then." They swapped chuckles over the line. "Now, back to my original question before you so rudely sidetracked me."

"All right. Yes! I got a card from him last week."

"Was it a mushy one?"

"You are the nosiest . . ."

"Best friend in all the world. Well?"

"No, it was funny. I need funny things in my life right now. That's why I called you, and now you say you can't come."

"I'll be there. You just keep those stores warmed up. We're going to do some serious shopping."

"See you in two weeks." Trish hung up the phone. Maybe she should call Rhonda every day. Maybe every hour.

Two weeks to wait. Ugh!

She checked her watch. Yes, time to stop by a card shop on her way home. Red was long overdue for an answer.

Reading the messages made her giggle out loud. She chose two funny ones for Red and then one for Rhonda. Writing them when she got home made her feel even better. How lucky she was to have such good friends in her life.

She thought a moment. Would Red be called a friend? Or a boyfriend? She fingered the cross on a chain around her neck. He'd given it to her to remember him by. She felt a shiver travel up her back. He really was a neat person. She touched her lips. The kisses had been nice. She giggled at the thought. Nice was not a good enough word. Rhonda was right.

That night she fell asleep in front of the television in the family room.

"Trish, it's 2:00 A.M." Martha shook Trish's shoulder. "Come on, get up to bed."

Trish blinked her eyes and sat up, trying to clear the

fog from her brain. The last she remembered was—she blinked again, she couldn't remember. "Uh, okay, thanks." She got up and stumbled up the stairs. She was asleep again before she pulled the covers up.

She was late for morning works.

"I'm sorry, guess I forgot to set my alarm." Trish slumped into the canvas chair.

Adam studied her face. "Looks to me like you shoulda slept about ten hours longer. But no matter, since three of the horses won't work this morning . . ."

Guilt made her bite her lip. She should've checked on the horses herself, at least the horses from Runnin' On Farm. "How's the mare?"

"About the same. We caught it in time, I think. We'll let Gatesby have a rest, too, just in case. Firefly seems fine, just warm her up this morning. She's in the Camino Diablo, the stakes for this afternoon." He rose to his feet. "Carlos has her ready, if you are."

Trish nodded. As ready as she'd ever be. She and Firefly slow-trotted the oval of the smaller track that lay close to the freeway. Cars were already slowing down in the morning rush-hour commute. The brassy sun peeped above the hills on the eastern side of San Francisco Bay, promising another hot day.

The filly tracked all the sights, sounds, and smells of the morning bustle, her ears and nostrils in constant motion. Trish leaned forward and stroked the shiny, red neck. "You're a beauty, you know that?" Firefly tossed her head and snorted.

Back at the barn when works were finished, Trish slumped back in her chair in the office. She crossed one booted foot over the other knee and picked off a piece of dried mud. A sigh escaped. She dropped her chin on her chest and rotated her head from side to side and back to front.

"Okay, what is it?"

"Huh?" She sat up straight.

"Something's on your mind." Adam leaned back in his chair, hands behind his head.

Trish ran her tongue over her lower lip. "Maybe—I—uh—I think you should put someone else up on Firefly today so she has a chance. She could win that—if . . ."

"If?"

Trish almost swallowed the words. "If I weren't riding her." The silence in the office was broken only by a huge fly buzzing at the window. "Adam, I can hardly even get 'em around the track. You could still get someone good, anyone would be better'n me."

When the silence stretched until Trish felt it quivering between them, she looked up to see Adam staring at her and shaking his head. "No, Trish. All you need is one good race and you'll be fine again. I think this afternoon will do it for you."

Trish pushed herself to her feet, shaking her head all the while. *I can't believe you did that,* she scolded herself on the way out to her car. *Maybe you should just chuck it all in and go home. Maybe you really are all washed up.* She leaned her forehead against the black cloth roof of her car. *Quitters never win and winners never quit.* How many times had her father said that through the years? If only he were here to say it now.

That afternoon Firefly pranced as if all the world applauded her personally. She trotted beside the pony rider, ears forward, neck arched, her coat almost the same crimson as that in Trish's silks. Crimson and gold, Runnin' On Farm colors and also those of Prairie High.

All ten entries walked into the gates without a problem. Trish gathered her reins and crouched forward, feeling Firefly settle on her haunches, ready for the gun.

The gates flew open. Firefly leaped forward. The horse on their right stumbled, crashed into Firefly, and hit the ground.

CHAPTER FOUR

Sheer willpower kept Firefly on her feet.

Trish wasn't sure whose willpower won as she clung to the filly's neck and held the reins firm. Another stride and the filly regained her balance. Two more strides and they were running straight. One more stride and Trish could feel a shudder in the right fore.

Firefly pulled up limping badly.

Trish vaulted to the ground. She ran a hand down the filly's leg, all the while murmuring the soothing sounds that calmed the horse. She could feel the swelling popping up right under her fingertips.

Slowly she led the limping filly out the gate and back to the barns. Adam caught up with her before she passed the first row of stalls.

"You should have . . ."

Adam held up a hand. "That could have happened to anybody."

Everything in Trish wanted to scream *I told you so!* She bit her tongue to keep the words back. Now her filly was injured and a strain like this could cause permanent damage. She thought of all the trouble they'd had with Spitfire's leg.

Her eyes felt scratchy along with her throat. After Carlos and Adam took over the care of the filly, she pulled a bottle of water out of the refrigerator and chug-a-lugged half of it. When would this cycle end?

Trish left the track and headed for the beach. While it was already late afternoon, she didn't have to meet her tutor until seven. Maybe, just maybe, she'd hear her song again and find the peace that went along with it. Traffic snaked to a crawl where Highway 92 crossed the Crystal Springs Reservoir and became a two-lane road. All the way up the winding, hilly road and down the ocean side to Half Moon Bay, the cars played either stop-and-go or slow-and-go.

Trish thrummed her fingers on the steering wheel. They were using up her time, her precious beach time. The sun hovered above the band of clouds hugging the horizon when she finally parked the car at Redondo Beach. She grabbed her blanket and pack from the trunk and slipped and slid down the rough trail.

Low tide exposed a wide expanse of beach as Trish trudged south toward her favorite spot. Since she and the gulls were the only visitors, she quickly spread her blanket and dropped into the middle of it.

Hugging her knees, she watched the gulls wheeling and dipping above her. Would her song come? She listened intently. The offshore breeze sent sand skittering before it and peppered the cliff behind her with its breath, loosening bits of rust and orange sandstone. It tugged on her hair, freeing tendrils from the braid down her back and blowing them into her eyes.

Impatiently she brushed them away. Where was her song? She tried humming a few bars but her throat closed.

Clutching her legs, Trish rocked forward and back, leaning her cheek on her jeans-clad knees. When she despaired of the song coming today, she hauled the journals out of her pack and, laying her father's beside her, dug out a pen and opened her own. The words poured out.

Why? Why is everything falling apart? I can't ride, I can't win, and most of all—I can't quit crying. This isn't fair! And when I'm not crying, I'm sleeping. Right now, I could lie down and in one minute be sound asleep. Maybe there's something terribly wrong with me. God, where are you? My dad always said you loved us no matter what. If this is what love is like, do me a favor. Go love someone else.

Trish stared at what she'd written. After blowing her nose, she picked up the pen again. *I want to have faith like my dad did.* She thought a bit, chewing on the end of her pen. *I guess. Do I really? Or do I just want to run away from the pain. I hurt so bad. My head aches, my nose is all plugged, and I'm so tired.*

"Please, God. Help me." She closed the book. Did she hear it? The song? "Dear God, I need those eagle's wings so bad."

She laid her book down and picked up her father's. Flipping through its pages, she saw verse after verse. One stuck out because it was underlined and circled. "Peace I leave with you, my peace I give unto you."

Trish felt like tearing the page out and ripping it to shreds to let the wind blow it away. Peace, there was no peace. She ground her teeth together. Fury, red hot and snapping sparks, blurred her vision. Her father said God lived up to His promises. Then why, even here at the beach today, was there was no peace? No song. No nothing.

The seagull dipped low and screeched at her.

"Shut up, you—you stupid bird." She threw a handful of sand at him, and with one last keening cry he tipped his wings and drifted off.

Never had she felt so alone. She looked up and down the beach. Totally empty. "Father, Dad, Daddy, help me!" The scream tore from her raw throat.

She dropped her head on the leather-covered journal and waited for the burning tears to flood her eyes. But they didn't. The burn continued.

Dry-eyed, she traced the embossed design of the cross on the front of the journal. "Please, please," she whispered, "please help me."

The sun disappeared behind the two-toned gray band of clouds swelling on the horizon. The wind, cold now, tugged and pulled at the figure sprawled on the square of red plaid spread on the shifting sand.

Trish sat up. She picked up her journal and stuck the pen in the pages, then placed it and her father's journal back in her blue pack. The song hadn't come. She stood, shook out the blanket, and folded it up. If peace came, what would it feel like? What did Jesus mean by "His peace"? She dug the journal out of the bag again and opened it, searching for the right page.

There. "Peace I leave with you, my peace I give unto you." The words hadn't changed. She read them again. And then her father's words that followed: *Father, God, I need your peace so desperately. Sometimes I am so afraid, and then I am comforted by your words. Peace means to me, right now, that you are in control and you will never let me go. Your love, your grace, are eternal, forever, and that means right now. Thank you, my Lord and my God.*

Trish shivered in the wind. Her dad had been afraid, too. She closed the book, keeping one finger in the place. "Thank you."

The tune floated in on the wind and curled around her bleeding heart.

When she reached the top of the cliff, she turned and looked over the white frosted breakers that crashed on the sand. One last ray of sun beamed up and painted the underside of the cloud in molten fire.

Trish hummed the song under her breath as she placed her bag and blanket in the trunk and removed her purse and schoolbag. She'd have time to grab a hamburger in Half Moon Bay before driving the curving road back up to the school.

"You look like something the cat wouldn't even drag in," Richard, her tutor, said when she dropped into the chair beside him.

"Thanks a lot. I needed to hear that." Trish smoothed the windblown hair back from her face. "Driving a convertible messes my hair. So what!"

"Nah, not just that. Your eyes are all red; you look like you've been crying for a week. What happened, your boyfriend dump you?"

Trish stared at him. "Since when do you care? All you've ever talked about is chemistry."

"Trish, that's what you pay me for."

"Well, you're not doing a very good job." Trish leaned back against the seat and crossed her ankles.

"Hey, your grades aren't my fault. You just aren't concentrating. I've watched you, your mind is off someplace far away. I think I'm just wasting my time."

"Fine. Quit then." Trish bit the inside of her cheek.

"No, we need to get to the bottom of this. You want to tell me what's wrong?"

Trish stared at him, her mind at war behind her burning eyes. "Not really."

Richard stared at her.

Trish stared back at him. One fat tear slipped from under her control and meandered down her cheek.

She clenched her fingers into fists until she could feel the nails biting into the palms of her hands. She would not back down.

Richard leaned forward and pulled a handkerchief from his back pocket. With a gentle touch, he wiped the tear away.

Trish's lip quivered. Her nose ran, followed by the tears she'd tried so hard to hold back.

Richard handed her the handkerchief. "Here. While you wipe your face, I'm going out in the hall to get us a couple of sodas. You like Diet Coke, right?" Trish nodded. "And then we'll talk, okay?" Trish nodded again.

The drink felt heavenly, both slipping down her throat and as the can pressed against her swollen eyes. "Thank you." She swallowed several more times and put the can to her cheek.

"My dad died the sixth of June." She took another drink. "Do you know much about thoroughbred horse racing?"

Richard shook his head.

"Well, I'm a jockey and . . ." Once having begun, Trish told the entire story, about their dream of winning with Spitfire, and about all the races they'd won. "And now I can't quit crying; I can't think; I can't do anything right anymore."

"Man, that's a bummer. No wonder you look sad, kinda spaced out all the time." Richard tugged at an earlobe that held a tiny diamond post. "Bummer."

"Yeah, you could call it that." Trish blew her nose again. "Sorry, I messed up your handkerchief. I'll take it home and wash it."

"No problem." Richard stared down at the chemistry books forgotten on the oak table in front of him. He looked up at her, seeming to stare through her eyes right into her brain. "I have something that can help you."

Trish stared back. "You do? Really?"

"Really." He dug in the pocket of his sweatshirt. "Here." He dropped four white capsules into her hand. "Uppers. They'll make you feel better. I promise."

CHAPTER FIVE

"Don't worry, you can't get hooked on a couple of uppers."

Trish's fingers trembled. "I—I know that."

"Well, I just thought they might help—like give you some energy and make you think better, maybe win a race or two. You know, even the doctors give these out."

Trish nodded. "I know. He—the doctor offered me some right after my dad died. Said it would help make things easier."

"Did you try it?"

Trish shook her head.

Richard looked at her and rolled his eyes. "Why not?"

"My dad always said we should depend on God for help, not pills and—stuff."

"Didn't he take the medicines the doctors told him to?"

Trish felt like her head was tied to a string. Nod yes, shake no. Her hands wouldn't quit trembling.

"Well, you like, think about it." He checked the clock on the wall. "We better get on the chemistry. I gotta be somewhere else in a while."

Trish shoved the pills in her pocket and opened her book. Maybe it was a good idea if those simple little white things could make her understand this stuff. But as Richard explained the formulas, her mind flitted off again. She fought to keep her eyes open. The warm room, full stomach, a droning voice—

"Trish, you're not paying attention!" Richard slammed his book shut.

Trish started. Her eyes flew open and her heart pounded. "You scared me."

He looked at her in disgust. "Take it from me, you *need* help." He pushed himself to his feet and gathered up his books. "And there's always more where those came from. All you have to do is ask."

Trish watched as he strode out the room, his blond ponytail curling down past his shoulders. He was trying to help, he really was. If only she could stay awake.

All you have to do is ask, kept ringing in her ears on the drive back to the condominium. That's what her father always said, too. He quoted the verse all the time, "Ask and you shall receive." Just ask. She snorted. She was sure he didn't mean ask for drugs.

But she *had* asked. She'd begged and pleaded for God to make her father well again. And He had—or the medicines had—for a time. But then her father died. The tears that always hovered just behind her eyelids pooled and blurred her vision. She wiped them away with the back of her hand.

And she'd prayed to win races. She had. And not just she and Spitfire. She'd won on plenty of other horses too. Her father always said she had a gift for understanding horses and getting the best out of them. So—had God taken the gift away?

She parked in the driveway at the hillside condo. Did God give gifts and take them away? Did He just answer prayers when He felt like it?

Wait a minute! She thumped her fist on the steering

wheel. *You said once you didn't believe in God anymore—remember? You said He wasn't real, but at the beach you were praying and begging again.*

The battle waged in her mind. One side yelled there was no God, and the other insisted God was her Father and loved her dearly. Trish dug her fingers into both sides of her scalp and rubbed until it hurt.

But who else can I turn to? What else is left? She pulled the pills from her pocket and stared at them in the light of the streetlamp. Would they *really* make her feel better? She stuffed them in her purse, grabbed her bags, and ran up the brick stairs.

She fell asleep after working only one chemistry problem. The thump of the book on the floor woke her so she could undress and crawl into bed. Another evening shot down. Would she never get this stuff?

———

The next morning, after working the horses that were healthy, Trish slumped into the chair in the office. She alternately sipped orange juice and munched a bagel. Adam and Carlos both favored coffee with their bagels, and Adam's was smeared liberally with cream cheese.

"You got any mounts in the next week or so?" Adam asked around a mouthful.

Trish shook her head. "Should bug my agent, but—I don't know—who'd want to hire me?"

Adam glared at her. "Well, there're lots of other jockeys who make up the races without winning."

"Yeah, right." She looked up in time to find Carlos glaring at her, too, sparks seeming to fly from his dark eyes.

"I think you should go home for a few days, then."

Adam set his coffee cup down and leaned forward. "If you leave tomorrow morning and come back Tuesday, you'll only miss one class."

"As if that makes any difference."

"Trish!"

"Okay, okay. I'm going. You want me to leave right now?"

Adam leaned back again with a grin on his face. "Martha will drive you to the airport. No sense paying for long-term parking if you don't have to."

"You had this all worked out, didn't you?" She stared from one smiling face to the other. "What about Firefly?"

"I think I can take care of her." It was the first time Trish had heard Carlos resort to sarcasm.

"I'm sorry, I didn't mean . . ."

"We know. Now get outta here."

Trish felt hope leap within her. Home—she was going home. She stopped at the first phone booth and called Runnin' On Farm. When the answering machine clicked on, she glanced at her watch. *Only 8:30.* She left a message. "I'm on my way home, first flight I can get. Call you as soon as I know. Oh, I hope you haven't gone for the day."

She called again from the house after making reservations. Same thing, just the answering machine.

A repeat at the airport.

"Don't worry, I'll keep trying," Martha assured her as they called the final boarding for Trish's flight. "You just have a good visit with your family. We'll miss you."

Trish returned Martha's hug and boarded the plane.

Halfway through the hour and a half flight, something set her butterflies off. Her stomach felt like just before a major race. She thought about the last time at home. Eyes closed, she leaned her seat back and remembered. Would the pain be as bad? She thought of the accident she'd had with her new car and that last hurried trip to Kentucky. No matter what, her father would not be there.

She pinched the bridge of her nose with her fingers and swallowed the scratchy lump in her throat. She leaned back in the seat and closed her eyes. But at least she would see the rest of her family, and Rhonda and Brad. She turned and drew her feet up onto the seat. Good thing she had a seat by herself.

Eventually she opened her eyes and stared out the window. Mount Hood, its snow covering slashed by granite faces after the summer melt, loomed below them to the left. Mount St. Helens glowed faintly in the haze to the north.

How would she get to the farm if no one was home? *Take a taxi, silly,* she told herself. *Or you could rent a car.* She shuffled along with the rest of the deplaning passengers. As she strode through the doors at the top of the ramp, the first thing she saw was her mother's face. David stood just behind her.

Trish ran the last few yards and threw her arms around her mother. "You came! You came!"

"Oh, my dear Tee, you didn't give us much notice." Their tears ran together as mother and daughter clung to each other.

"I drove like a bat out of . . ." David sniffed along with the others.

Trish transferred her bear hug to her brother's neck. "I'm just so glad you're here. Feels like a year or two since I've been home."

"Well, not quite that long." David set her back on her

feet. "You ever think of planning ahead?"

Trish shook her head. "Adam said I should take a break—Firefly nearly did—and get outta there. I didn't argue too much. Oh, I've been so homesick!" She hugged her mother again.

"You got any more than this?" When Trish shook her head, David and Marge picked up the bags, and with Trish in the middle, the three headed for the parking lot.

Trish caught up on all the latest news on the drive across the I–205 bridge and through the small town of Orchards on the way to Runnin' On Farm. Trish kept one eye on the scenery to see any changes, and her mind on the conversation.

"But wouldn't it have been easier to go back to WSU?" she asked at one point when David was telling her about Tucson.

"Yeah, but after Dad and I talked to the people in Kentucky about the equine program in Tucson, that's all I wanted to do. You have to admit I have some experience in doctoring horses by now."

"So much for the small animal practice you talked about, huh?"

"I think caring for horses is in my blood. Since I'm too big to ride and you'll want to do all the training eventually . . ."

"What about me?" Marge asked. "I'm getting better and better with the babies. You'll see, Tee."

"She is. Who'd ever dream that *our* mother would be down training Miss Tee and Double Diamond. And she's good."

"As you said, brother mine, must be in the blood." Trish turned to grin at her mother. "I'm really proud of you."

"Patrick's talking about attending some of the sales after you get back. Like the yearling sale down at Santa Anita this fall." Marge clasped her daughter's hand. "What do you think?"

"You want to expand?" Trish could feel her chin hit her chest.

"I'm thinking about it. We have a lot of talking to do."

Trish kept waiting for the pain to strike again. But it didn't. Maybe riding in the new van helped since her father had never been in it.

When they turned into the drive of Runnin' On Farm, Trish felt her heart leap. Caesar, the farm's sable collie, met them halfway up the drive, dancing and barking his greeting.

Everything looked the same as usual. Pink, purple, and white petunias lined the sidewalk up to the front door and drifted down the sides of the two tall clay pots flanking either side of the steps. Lush rosebushes fronted the house, covered in blossoms of pink, yellow, and deep red, with all the shades in between.

Caesar planted both front feet on Trish's shoulders as soon as she stepped out of the car. "Down, you goofy dog!" Trish grabbed his ruff with both hands, shaking and hugging him at the same time. "I think you missed me."

Caesar whimpered, and did his best to make sure Trish's face was cleaned of all traces of California.

"I want to go to the barns first, okay?"

"Why am I not surprised?" Marge locked arms with Trish. "Patrick is off looking at a mare we heard about. She's in foal to Seattle Slew also. You know how much your father thought of that stud."

Trish swallowed a gulp of surprise. Was this really

her mother talking? "You might buy her?"

"We're thinking about it. We have a lot to talk about, things that need discussing if Runnin' On Farm is to be managed wisely."

David poked Trish in the ribs and gave her an I-told-you-so grin. Trish poked him back.

"Wow, look at Patrick's trailer . . ."

"Manufactured home," David drawled out his bit of information. "They don't call them trailers or mobile homes anymore."

"Whatever. Looks like it's been there forever."

"I think he loves flowers and landscaping as much as he does horses. Says he has to have something to keep him busy while half the string is in California." Marge stuck her hands in the back pockets of her jeans. "The whole place looks good, don't you think?"

"Yeah, you even painted the barns."

"I did that," David said. "Amazing what a little extra money can do, along with a lot of elbow grease. Brad helped me."

"And me." Marge grinned at her daughter. "I was the go-fer." She grabbed Trish's hand again. "Come on, see my babies."

Marge whistled as they rounded the long, low row of stalls and headed down the lane to the pastures. The mares had returned from breeding and now grazed peacefully in the deep rich grass. Marge whistled again and the two youngsters in a paddock of their own thundered up to the fence.

"Oh, they've grown! Just think, Miss Tee is almost a year old." The colt and filly pushed at each other to get to Marge's offered carrot bits. When Trish extended her hand, the filly snuffled and lipped her fingers. "Oh, you sweety, you're just getting prettier and prettier. Look how red you are." Trish rubbed up the filly's cheek and behind her ears.

Marge entertained Double Diamond with the same kind of motions. Both the horses stood quietly, Miss Tee sniffing Trish's arm, shoulder, and hair.

"Mom, you've sure calmed them down." Trish kissed the filly on her soft nose. "See ya later, kid." The babies followed along the fence line as the three strolled to the next paddock, with the dog that never moved an inch from Trish's side.

"I enjoy the time with them, it's like I'm closer to Hal this way. It's funny, all those years I think I was a bit jealous of the time he spent with the horses and the way you kids idolized your father. And then I worried, too, of course."

"About everything you could think of and then some," David said with a teasing grin.

Trish forced a smile on her face to match theirs. Her mother had changed so much; was she still the same person? "And you really don't worry anymore?"

"I save it for the seventh Tuesday of the month." Marge leaned her crossed arms on the mare's paddock fence. "But really, Tee, I try to turn everything over to God immediately. And when the worries come back, I give them up again. I win most of the time."

"Wow." Trish shook her head. She stared out at the mares. Old gray Dan'l grazed with them. She rolled her bottom lip tightly over her teeth to whistle for him, but the quivering in her chin flubbed the effort. She scrubbed the back of her hand across her mouth and tried again. This time the high-low-high tone reached the horses' ears.

While all the animals lifted their heads, the gray flung his up and stared toward the fence. Trish whistled again. Dan'l broke into a lope and charged to the fence, his mane and tail feathering in the breeze. He skidded to a halt, nickering and tossing his head. When he reached Trish, he nosed her face, blew, and whuffled all at the same time.

Trish buried her face in his mane. "Oh, Dan'l." The old gelding had been her confidant and comforter for years. As she hugged the horse, she could feel her mother's arm around her shoulder.

David handed her a handkerchief when she stepped back.

"Sorry." She blew her nose and mopped her eyes.

"No, don't be. I'm just so grateful you can cry now. That tough shield you put up kept us all apart. We couldn't help you." Marge turned and leaned against the fence. "Oh, Tee, I prayed so hard for this."

"Yeah, I think she even worried about you, in spite of her good intentions."

"Wash your mouth with soap." Marge lightly punched her son on the arm. "Although I have to admit, sometimes the praying versus worrying line is mighty narrow."

Dan'l leaned his head over Trish's shoulder, settling in for a good scratching. Trish obliged, murmuring love words to him every once in a while.

"Don't be afraid or ashamed of the tears, Trish. There's a verse in the Old Testament that talks about God saving our tears in a bottle. That's how important they are."

"Well, He better have a mighty big bottle, the way I've been blubbering." Trish gave Dan'l a last pat and pushed away from the fence. "Come on, I'm thirsty for a drink of real water. That stuff down there isn't fit for drinking." Dan'l nickered as they left. "Maybe I should take a jug back with me."

Patrick clamped his hand to his heart when he walked into the house that evening. "Lord love ye, lass, what a sight for these poor old eyes." Trish met him in the middle of the room and fell into his hug.

"Poor old eyes, my foot." She sniffed—again—and stepped back to study him. "Patrick, you look wonderful. I think living in the rainy state agrees with you."

"That is does, lass." He studied her back. "Wisht I could say the same for you."

"You don't like my California tan?" Trish put her fingertips to her cheeks.

"Nay, it's not the tan." He nodded, squinting his eyes and clicking his tongue. "But I think you'll be better now."

"Better than what?"

"Just better, is all."

The evening passed more easily than Trish had imagined. She caught herself laughing as David, the David she used to know and love, teased them all in turn. He kept digging at her when she tried to sidestep their questions, until she confessed all. Her loneliness, the constant falling asleep, the fears of never riding well again, never winning. She told them everything—except about the pills she still had in her purse.

Should she—could she—tell them that?

CHAPTER SIX

They'd surely think California had turned her into a druggie.

Why hadn't she just flushed the stupid things so she wouldn't have to feel guilty about carrying them around? Maybe she'd do that later.

But she didn't do it before she crawled into bed, her own bed, in her own room. Her wandering gaze stopped at the empty bulletin board above her desk where she and her father had pinned up 3×5 cards with Bible verses on them.

Why had she ripped them down and dumped them in the trash?

She pressed her knuckle against her teeth, trying to remember which verses had been up there. A knock on the door broke her concentration.

"Trish." Her mother poked her head in. "Okay if I come in?"

"Sure." Trish shifted over in the bed so there was room for her mother to sit. "What's up?"

Marge sat down on the edge of the bed and turned so she could look at Trish. "I just want to tell you how happy I am to have you home. You have no idea how I've missed you."

"Yeah, I know. Only I think I didn't figure out what

part of my problem was until last week. Then when I admitted I was homesick, I couldn't get it out of my mind."

"You know something else?"

"What?"

"You're *you* again, not that angry person who was ready to tear anybody and everybody limb from limb." Marge brushed a tendril of hair back from Trish's cheek.

"Was I that bad?"

"Uh-huh. I know you think I'm crazy, but when I see you cry . . ."

"You cry, too."

"I know, but some of those are tears of gratitude. I think I'm walking by sight now, not just faith, faith that you're getting better."

Trish thought of the pills in her purse. "Mom, I . . ." A silence invaded the room.

"What?"

"Ah, nothing. Just sometimes I feel like a yo-yo, and whoever's pulling the string isn't very good at it."

Marge smiled. "That's a pretty good description."

The silence stretched again.

"Are you so tired all the time you can hardly stay awake?" Trish asked.

"I was. That's part of the grieving. Takes a lot of energy. I slept a lot. Prayed a lot. Cried a lot. No particular order." Marge clasped her hands around one raised knee. "And I talked with Pastor Mort. He gave me Bible verses that helped. You might want to try that while you're home."

"Maybe I will." A yawn cracked her jaw.

Marge copied the jaw cracking, then rose to her feet. She leaned over and kissed Trish on the cheek. "Good-night, my dear. Always remember, God loves you and so do I."

Trish wrapped her arms around her mother's neck and clung. "Good-night, Mom."

When Trish awoke in the morning, she lay in her bed looking around her room in the early light. Her clothes all hung neatly in the closet; the racing posters she'd collected were on the walls, the framed pictures of her and Spitfire in the winner's circles were there—it was her room. She stretched and yawned, then stretched her arms way over her head and twisted her body from side to side.

What was different? Besides being at home. She thought of the night she'd just slept through—no dreams, no nightmares, no lying awake thinking of failures. Just pure, peaceful rest. The verse flashed through her mind. "Peace I leave with you, my peace I give unto you." Was this what it meant?

She lay there, savoring the thought. She'd prayed for peace, hadn't she? Or had she just begged for help? Was God really answering her prayers?

She threw the covers back and went to stand at the window. Sunshine, no clouds—in Vancouver, Washington? God must indeed be welcoming her home. All the pastures were green, not brown like the hillsides of California. She inhaled. The rosebushes under her window welcomed her with their fragrance.

Patrick's whistled tune floated up on the breeze. She could hear her mother singing in the kitchen. Caesar barked at something off in the woods. All the sounds of home. Trish felt like a grin all over.

She glanced at the clock. *Six-thirty.* She'd really slept in. After pulling on jeans and a T-shirt, she grabbed her boots, stopped in the bathroom to brush her teeth and hair, and trotted into the kitchen.

"Thought maybe you'd sleep in." Marge turned from the sink. "Breakfast will be ready about eight."

Trish looked at the dough spread on the counter. "Cinnamon rolls?" Marge nodded. "Wow!" Trish gave her mother a two-armed hug and started from the room. She turned and backpedaled. "Hey, I've turned into a bagel connoisseur. We'll have some when you come down to California." She slid open the sliding glass door to the deck and plunked herself down on one of the cedar benches while she pulled on her boots.

All the fuchsia baskets dripped with flowers in shades of purple, pink, white, and red. She sat perfectly still as a hummingbird clicked his way past and dined on the hanging blossoms. Her father had loved the hummingbirds. Trish felt a catch in her throat. So often they'd sat together just like this to watch the flying jewels sipping at their flowers.

She had the distinct impression that if she could turn quickly enough, she would see him—her father smiling at her and walking beside her. The feeling persisted. Down at the barns when she checked each stall. In the tack room where they'd so often cleaned gear. Patrick sat there now, right outside the door, soaping a bridle.

"Top o' the morning, lass. You wouldn't be looking for a mount now, would you?" He laid the bridle in his lap. "Dan'l would love a lap or two around the track, if you've a mind."

"Thanks, but not today. I'm on vacation, remember?"

"That you are." He watched as she inspected the office.

If she closed her eyes, she could see her father sitting in his chair. She opened them quickly. He was gone. She waited, waited for the crashing pain to leap through her again. Instead, she heard a tuneless whistle—or did she?

Caesar caught up with her when she visited the foaling stall. She scratched his ears while she waited in the empty box stall. Less than a year ago, on her birthday, they'd come home from dinner out and found Miss Tee just getting her spindly legs under her to struggle to her feet.

Trish wandered down the lane to the paddocks. Miss Tee and Double Diamond rushed up to see her, and Dan'l nickered for his turn to be scratched.

"Thank you, Father, thank you." She rested her forehead against Dan'l's warm neck. What words could she say? None were enough.

When she turned for the house, she waited a moment. Such a strange feeling, but such a good one. A metallic blue Mustang was parked in the drive. When she opened the front door, she could hear Brad and Rhonda bantering in the dining room.

Trish paused for another moment. Her father's recliner looked like he'd just left it to go into another room. His Bible lay open on the lampstand beside it.

"I thought you had a show this weekend." Trish rounded the corner and attacked her two friends.

"I do, I do." Rhonda spun around and grabbed Trish around the waist. "We leave in an hour but I couldn't turn down your mom's cinnamon rolls. Oh, Trish, I'm so glad you're here!"

"Even though you won't be." She turned to hug Brad, the tall fourth of their four musketeers. The four young people had been best friends since grade school. "Seems like forever since I've seen you guys."

"Well, we haven't been anywhere. How ya doing, kid?" Brad swung her off her feet. When he set her down, he cupped her face in his hands. "You're better." It was a statement, not a question.

How could they all tell? Was she wearing a sign or something?

"Come and eat!" Marge set a platter of scrambled eggs with bacon on one end of the table and one of cinnamon rolls at the other. "David, you say grace." They all slid into their seats, Patrick where Hal used to sit, and held hands while David said the blessing.

When Trish looked up, a tiny barb of resentment for Patrick usurping her father's chair dug at the edge of her mind. She cringed when she remembered the blow-up last time she had been home. No, she told herself, no more. Again, there was that feeling that if she turned quickly enough she would see her father smiling and nodding at her. The peace stayed with her.

Trish took her first bite of homemade cinnamon roll and rolled her eyes in ecstasy. "Mom, no one bakes like you do. You should open a shop and sell these. You'd make a million in California."

"As if I had any desire to move to California. Here, Brad, have some more. I know you have a big day ahead of you." Marge passed the plate of rolls again.

"Why, what's happening today?" Trish asked after a bite of scrambled eggs.

"Brad has a job," Rhonda answered.

"Yeah, they laid me off at Runnin' On Farm." Brad waved his fork in the air. "So I had to go to work for my dad during the week. I run the stop-and-go signs on his road repair jobs, and on Saturdays I work at the cinema over at the mall. I get to see all the movies for free."

"Two jobs?"

"Yeah, college costs money."

"I thought you were going to Clark, and you got a scholarship."

"I did and I am, but WSU is expensive so I'm saving ahead." He reached for another cinnamon roll. "Trish is right, Mrs. E, you oughta go into business."

Marge shook her head, her smile the kind that mothers give their harebrained kids' ideas. "I have a business already. Remember, you worked for us. And will again when the racing string comes home, if you can fit us into your busy schedule."

"Hey, that's right. And this way you can make cinnamon rolls just for us."

"And chocolate chip cookies and peanut butter cookies," Trish and Rhonda said together.

"And I'll be so far away, no one will bake for me." David adopted a soulful look.

"Yeah, right!" Trish sent him a pretend glare. "Like you never got any care packages when you were at WSU."

"Oh, that's right." He raised one finger in the air. "But I had to fight for my rights. Whenever a box came from home, every guy on my floor dropped in to visit. Had to hide the goodies under my bed."

"Phew! Along with all the dirty socks and sweaty underwear. Yuk!"

"Okay, okay," Marge said, laughing along with them. "I promise to bake—when I have time."

"You didn't want cookies anyway." Trish got her last dig in. She looked over at Patrick and caught the telltale sheen in his eyes. He smiled back at her and winked. Was he a mind-reader like her father?

The day flew by like the view from a car traveling 60 miles an hour. Trish watched her mother work both Miss Tee and Double Diamond on the lunge line.

"You've taught them good manners," she said as she helped her mother brush the filly down. "This baby seems so willing to learn, she'll be easy to train."

"Yes, I think so. And does she ever love to run." Marge stopped her brushing. "You remember how much your father loved to work with the babies? He always said that was the fun part of training thoroughbreds."

"I know. He'd be so proud of you, Mom."

"I know he is. Trish, I don't think heaven is some faraway place. I think he knows what's going on and—well, sometimes he seems so close."

"I've felt it at home this time, too. Like if I look around quick enough, he'll be there." Trish rolled her lips together. "Mom, I'm so glad to be home."

They finished the filly and started on the colt. Trish tickled the colt's nose so he twitched his whiskers. "You think Dad could be a guardian angel?"

"If there is any way to be one, I'm sure he would be."

That evening the Evanstons and Patrick adjourned to the living room after a steak dinner broiled to perfection on the barbecue and devoured out on the deck.

"That was so good, Mom. And David, you're a super chef, almost as good as Dad. I haven't had home-cooked food since the last time I was here."

"Don't you eat with Adam and Martha?" Marge settled into her rocking chair.

"I'm never there at mealtime. Leave before breakfast, lunch at the track, and then grab something quick before class." Trish shrugged. "It's not their fault. Martha sometimes has a plate saved for me, but I hate to put her out.

They're so good to me anyway."

"I know. That makes having you down there easier for me." Marge leaned back in her chair. "How about we bring Trish up to date on the stuff we've been talking about. We're going to have to make some decisions soon."

"What stuff?"

Marge gave Patrick the nod. "You tell her."

"We've been looking for some more horses, like the mare I saw yesterday. I think we should buy her. I saw her filly from last year. Looks real good. In fact, we could probably get the filly too. Anson pretty much wants to sell out. What with Long Acres closing and the trouble at Portland Meadows, he says he'd just as soon get out now."

"What trouble at the Meadows?" Trish interrupted as soon as he paused.

"You know, more of the same. One day the place is up for sale and the next they're closing down." David shook his head in disgust. "Why they can't manage that place better, I'll never know."

Trish poked him in the ribs. "Maybe we oughta buy the track."

Marge rubbed her chin with one finger. "I've thought about it."

"What!" Trish and David stared at their mother and then each other.

"Your mother has some good ideas," Patrick said. "You know she's been the business manager for your father all these years with such a tight budget, now she— you all have to think and invest wisely."

"Maybe I should be taking a business course instead of chemistry." Trish slumped back, one ankle crossed over the other knee. She thought of the incredible amount of money sitting in her bank account. She hadn't thought about investing it. She didn't even have time to spend much of it.

"What if Adam and I see a good claimer? Should I go for it?" She looked from Patrick to her mother and back again. "Sarah's Pride was a good deal."

"We'll think about it. We'll probably go to the yearling sales this year too."

Trish went to bed that night in a total state of shock. Her mother was not only not thinking of selling the farm, but she planned to expand. She stared at the pictures of the winner's circles. *Oh, Dad, if only you were here to enjoy all this. You worked so hard for it, and now that your dream has come true, you're missing out.*

Trish woke in the morning to gray skies, but the gray couldn't dim the wonder she felt. Another night without nightmares. She thought back to the discussion the night before. How exciting! She threw back the covers and bounded out of bed.

"Think I'll take Dan'l for a ride," she said as she entered the kitchen.

"I think that'll be fine after church." Her mother set her coffee cup down on the counter. "You going down to help the guys with chores?"

Trish nodded. "I'd really like to go riding."

"I know. How long since you've been to church?"

"Ahh . . ." Trish leaned over to pull on her right boot.

"Since the last time you were home?" Marge picked up her cup and studied her daughter over the rim.

"Ummm . . ." She pulled on her left.

"Martha and Adam don't go to church?"

"Depends on the schedule at the track." *You could have gone if you wanted to,* Nagger whispered. *How many races have you had on Sundays anyway?* "Don't worry, Mom. I'll be ready on time." Trish gave up gracefully. Much as she didn't really want to go to church, she didn't want to cause a fracas with her mother either.

But she had a bad feeling on the drive to their church in Orchards. And it didn't get any better when they parked in the parking lot. *I think I'll just stay here*, she wanted to cry out as they all got out of the car.

David waited at the open van door after Marge stepped down. "You gonna wait all day?" He peered in at his sister.

Trish chewed on her cuticle. She took a deep breath and let it out. Even so, her knees turned to mush when her feet met the ground.

Patrick took her arm and tucked it in his. "You'll be fine, lass," he whispered in her ear.

Trish stared straight ahead. She walked up the six outside steps and through the door. She shook hands with the greeters, hoping they didn't feel her shaking.

When she sat down in the pew, she kept her gaze glued on her hands, clenched together in her lap. The tears prickled at the first hymn. She bit them back, her teeth grinding together in the effort.

If she didn't look at Pastor Mort, she could handle it. She tried to block out the words he read from the Bible. She used to be so good at blocking things out. She tried to think of racing Spitfire, of the feel of him thundering for the finish.

That was worse.

She tried to make her mind blank. Utter failure.

Pastor Mort entered the pulpit. He waited for the last feet to stop shuffling, the last cough and rustle.

Trish scrunched her eyes closed.

"Grace and peace from God our Father and the Lord Jesus Christ." The voice rolled over the congregation and invaded Trish's heart. The dammed-up tears choked her. Trish pushed herself to her feet and strode down the aisle.

CHAPTER SEVEN

God, I can't do this!

"Can I get you something?" An usher touched Trish on the shoulder as she stood at the back of the church.

"No, no thank you." Trish blew her nose in a soggy tissue. "I'll be fine." *No you won't.* Nagger even came to church with her. *Unless you give it up, you'll never be fine again.* Trish hiccuped on a sob.

"Here." The man handed her his handkerchief.

When Trish's brain reformed after mushing during the tears, she thought back to what Nagger had said. *Give what up?* She sank down on a chair and took a shaky breath. She'd wait for her family here.

Pastor Mort closed his sermon with the benediction. "The Lord bless you and keep you . . ." The words bathed Trish's wounded feelings in the balm of love. ". . . and give you His peace."

That's what it was. The feeling was back again. Trish sighed in relief.

The guitars played the opening chords of the closing hymn. At the sound of her theme song, Trish fled from the church before she broke down completely. The congregation's singing followed her out the door. "And He will raise you up on eagle's wings . . ."

She huddled on the backseat of the van, her knees

drawn up to her chest, her hands over her face. The tears poured through her fingers and soaked her hair. Finally, after what seemed eons, she pushed herself upright. She slumped against the seat, too drained to sit up. Lifting her hands to push her hair back took all her energy.

A red and black handkerchief, big enough to be a bandanna, appeared from her right. She turned enough to see Patrick sitting on the step, extending the cloth.

She took it and blew her nose for the millionth time. Her nose was raw, her throat was raw, and her feelings the most raw of all.

When she put the handkerchief down, he handed her a cup of water.

"Should I pour this over my head or down my throat?"

"Whichever. Looks to me like you're wet enough already." A smile wreathed his face, telling her without a word that he understood, and that he appreciated her attempt at humor. "Aye, lass, when ye can laugh at yerself, ye be on the way."

"On the way to what?" Trish sniff-sniffed on a breath.

"To learning to deal with the blows life gives ye. Yer takin' this one young-like, but now I know you'll be makin' it."

Trish finished the water in the cup. "What makes you so sure?"

"I just know, lass, I just know. Must be that faith that Pastor Mort talked about today."

"But, Patrick, the last couple of days, I thought this was all over. I felt good again for the first time in—in, I don't know how long. And then to fall apart like this . . ."

"But don't you see, the falling apart, as you call it, is part of the giving up." His waving hands punctuated his words.

"But, Patrick, you keep saying give it up ... but I don't know what I'm supposed to give up." She strangled the handkerchief.

"The wall, lass, that tough spirit so full of anger no one could come near you."

"What I want to give up is the black hole I live in all the time." The words faded away to a whisper.

"You will."

David and Marge joined Patrick at the side of the mini-van. When Trish opened her eyes again, most of the other cars had left the parking lot. She looked back to the church entry. Pastor Mort had only one more family to greet.

Trish drew a staggery breath again. She sniffed and wiped her nose. "Think I'll go see Pastor Mort. Is that okay? You guys in a hurry?"

Marge smiled through the tears that brightened her eyes. "No, Tee, take your time."

Pastor Mort, the sun glistening on the bald top of his head, was just turning to go back into the church when Trish called to him. The smile on his face set her lip quivering again.

"Ah, Trish, I'm so glad to see you." He met her at the bottom of the steps.

When she took his extended hand, he pulled her into a hug, then leaned back to study her face. "I could tell how hard it was for you to sit there, even as long as you did."

Tears pooled in her eyes again. How could there be any tears left in her body? "How come church is so hard? I get so tired of crying."

"Yes, I know." He sat down on the step and tugged on her hand to join him. "So many people tell me that.

I guess it's because we're more vulnerable in God's house. I think He uses that time to draw us closer to himself so He can take the pain away."

"But it only hurts more."

"No, you only feel it more. And the more you let the feelings out, the easier it will get. Besides, what better place to fall apart than with all these people who love you and want to help any way they can? You gave them a chance to pray for you, to reach out in love. And near as I can figure, that's what being part of the family of God is all about."

Trish leaned her chin on her hand on her bent knees. "I tried not to come today."

"I'm not surprised, but I'm sure glad you're here."

"You *really* think I'm better?" The thought of the pills in her purse flashed through her mind.

"Yes, I do."

"Do you believe in angels?"

"Of course."

"My mom and I wondered if Dad could be an angel."

"I don't know the answer to that, Trish. But I do know that if there were any way possible for him to help you, he would."

"He's all better now, isn't he?" She rolled her lips to keep from crying out loud.

"Yes, Trish, he is."

When she looked up, Pastor Mort was wiping away tears, too. Trish held up Patrick's soaked handkerchief. "I think I should buy shares in Kleenex."

"Oh, Trish." Pastor Mort laughed. He blew his nose and chuckled again. "Yes, my dear, you're definitely better."

"Well, I hope you're right." She rose to her feet and

extended her hand. "Thanks. See you next time I'm home."

"Bless you, child." He squeezed her hand, then held her in a firm embrace.

———

When they got home, Trish felt like someone had pulled the plug and let out all the bath water. *Drained* was the only word that applied. She sat down on her bed to remove her shoes. She eyed the pillow. Maybe if she lay down for just a minute she'd feel like going in to help her mother make Sunday dinner. Then maybe David would help her with her chemistry.

Her mother shook her two hours later. "Come on Trish, dinner's ready."

"Okay, be there in a minute."

David shook her fifteen minutes later. She hadn't even heard him come into her room.

"Okay, okay." She pushed her hair back from her face. "What's wrong?"

"Trish, time to eat. Mom came and called you fifteen minutes ago."

"Nah." She swung her feet off the bed and sat up. Her gaze focused on the clock. "Why'd you guys let me sleep so long?"

David thumped her on top of her head. "Just come and eat."

When she shuffled out to the table, she saw Brad in his usual place. "Hi, sleepyhead."

"Hi." Trish blinked once and then again. She just couldn't wake up. " 'Scuse me a moment. I need a cold-water treatment." When she returned after dousing her face in cold water, she could at least see straight. "Now, what all did I miss out on?"

David bowed his head. "Father, we thank you for this food, for our family and friends, and we ask you to help Trish work through this bad time. Amen."

Trish had a hard time swallowing. Here was David praying for her, too. And saying grace just like her father used to.

"You do that good, Davy boy, just like Dad."

"Thanks, he taught us well."

Marge watched her daughter; two little worry lines creased the space between her eyebrows. "Trish, is this typical, falling asleep like that?"

"No, not quite the same. This time was like someone hit me over the head. Usually I just nod off. My brain turns to dandelion fluff and blows away." She glanced from face to face around the table. "Hey, that's a joke, guys. I'm tired a lot, can't concentrate, that's all."

"Okay, but it might be a good idea to see a doctor and get checked out. Maybe you're anemic or something."

"M-o-m." Trish felt the hairs on the back of her neck rise. This felt too much like the times when Marge drove everyone nuts with her worrying. Back when they had a hard time getting along. Were those times returning?

Marge raised her hands in a gesture of surrender. "Don't panic, I'm not worrying. It's just that sometimes parents have to insist on what they think is right—and this is one of those times."

"But I leave tomorrow afternoon."

"There are no doctors in California?"

Trish looked up at her mother with a lopsided grin and a shake of the head. "I'll ask Martha for the name of one."

"Good idea, Trish," Patrick said from his end of the table.

"Whew! Glad that's over." David nudged Brad, who also wore a look of relief. "No World War III this time," he added under his breath.

"David?" Trish asked so sweetly that bees would think it was honey. "How about if I just pour this glass of water on your head now?"

"Whoa . . . we better watch out!" David and Brad swapped big-brother smirks.

The glow in her middle reminded Trish that this was the kind of stuff she missed the most.

––––––––

"How's the chemistry coming?" David asked that evening after chores.

"You don't really want to know." Trish stared glumly at the book on her lap.

"Have you prayed about it?"

She shot him a look of surprise. "You sound just like Dad."

"I'll take that as a compliment, even though right now I don't think you meant it that way. But he was right. Ask for help. Ask God to make this stuff clear to you. If He could create the world, what's a little chemistry?"

"If He created it, He understands it," Trish muttered. "It's getting it through my thick head that's the problem."

"True. But I thought you got a tutor."

"I did. Richard keeps trying, but he says I just don't concentrate enough. Seems to be the story of my life lately." Trish chose not to mention the earring, the ponytail, and the pills. Instead she told her brother about the hours she'd spent studying and the crummy test and quiz scores she'd gotten.

"David, I just don't like chemistry," she whispered so her mother wouldn't hear.

"So *pass* it and be done with it," he hissed back.

"I need a B on the final to pull a C. You know what that's going to do to my grade average?"

"So—when all else fails, *pray*. What have you got to lose?"

Trish dug her elbow into his rib cage. "Thank you so very much."

But when she went to bed that night, Trish knelt on her rug and rested her head on her clasped hands. "God, I don't know where else to turn. As David says, you're it. Your Word says I should ask and receive. I'm asking—for help with my chemistry, and for—to keep me awake when I need to study." She thought for a moment. "And please get me out of the pit I've been in. Amen."

She climbed into bed. "And thank you for bringing me home."

Early the next morning, Trish and David, Marge and Patrick drove north in the mini-van.

Trish yawned in the backseat. "So much for sleeping in. You really think these horses are worth buying, huh, Patrick?"

"That I do, lass."

"Patrick's looked a lot around Portland and southern Washington," Marge said. "Your dad always said Patrick had an eye for a good horse, like a man for a pretty woman." Marge copied Trish's yawn. "Excuse me. Now look what you've started."

Patrick handed a sheaf of papers to Trish. "Look at

these and see what you think."

Trish flipped through copies of registration papers, bloodlines, and racing statistics. "Which ones are you thinking of?"

"That mare in foal to Slew, the yearling colt, and possibly one of the fillies. Depends on how much your mom wants to spend."

"That would give us three to train this fall. But where would we race them if Portland Meadows doesn't open?"

"California, I suppose." Marge took the pages about the mare. "We thought about talking to Adam if we need to. He could race them down south if we have any good enough."

"They just better get the Meadows running." Trish deciphered bloodlines while she kept track of the conversation. How strange to be having this kind of discussion with her mother.

They left the I–5 freeway at Chehalis, heading west through dairy country. Acres of white board fences bounding knee-deep pastures announced the horse farm before the sign at the driveway.

"Is the farm for sale too?" Trish asked. "This is beautiful." Babies kicked up their heels in a pasture to their right and a couple of yearlings raced along the fence beside them. Up ahead, on a slight rise, the house reminded Trish of those in Kentucky—white, tall pillars in front, and an air of history.

The barns even sported cupolas like many of those in Kentucky. "Why are they selling their horses?"

"Anson Danielson is getting up in years, and with Seattle closing and the trouble at Portland, he feels it's time to retire. They have no living children to take over, so they're selling. Patrick got wind of it, and because he knew Mr. Danielson years ago, called him. You know the rest."

"Aren't they having a dispersal sale?"

"Not if they can get decent prices without it." David glanced at Trish in the rearview mirror. "His wife has been sick and he doesn't want all the hassle."

Dad should be here doing this, Trish thought as Patrick greeted the man. She sighed and followed the others. The horses were all that Patrick had said.

Trish walked around the mare, checking confirmation as her father had taught her. She tickled the little filly's nose, and felt down her legs. Her dad said it was hard to tell anything at this age, but the filly had the look of a winner. The way she carried her head, you could tell she liked to show off. She had both the body and the bloodlines for speed.

But there was something about the colt. What would her dad have said? This just wasn't fair. He should be here. He worked all his life for this dream, and now he was gone. Trish tried to think what he would say and do. First, her father would be happy, with the day and the trip and the horses. He had liked nothing better than visiting horse farms.

She squinted her eyes to think better. Then he would have studied the horses. Really looked them over.

She leaned her chin on her fists on the top of the board fence. While she watched the horses grazing in the field, she could almost feel her dad standing beside her. What was it about the colt?

"So, what do you think?" Marge leaned on the fence beside her daughter.

"Whatever."

"No, this has to be a family decision. If you have doubts, say so."

"I wish Dad were here," Trish whispered.

"Yeah, me too."

They watched the grazing animals a while longer before Marge turned and propped her elbows on the fence. "Okay now?"

Trish nodded. "Better." And surprisingly, she was.

"We better get a move on or you'll be late for your flight. We don't have to make a decision today, I just thought you might like to see them first."

"But if we don't, someone else could outbid us?"

"There's that."

"Then I'd say yes on the mare and filly, and I don't know on the colt. Something about him bothers me. I tried to figure out what Dad would have said but I'm not sure."

Patrick and David joined them at the fence. "You're right, lass, about the colt. It's in the way he moves. No sense in buying a future problem."

"But he could outgrow it?" David asked.

"Maybe."

"Then we agree? The mare and filly?" Marge looked to each of them in turn. At their nods, she dug in her purse and pulled out her checkbook. "I think your dad would be proud of us right now."

Trish gulped as her mother signed the check and handed it to Mr. Danielson. They now owned two new horses. Amazing what money could do. She dozed off on the way home in spite of the discussion about transporting and training the new additions.

They got home just in time for her to grab her things and load the van.

"Now, you're stopping to see me on your way to Tucson," she made David promise. "And, Patrick, you and

Mom are coming down to see Firefly run. Maybe we'll have a horse or two for you to look at by then."

"Aye, lass. That we will," Patrick agreed. "Say hello to Adam for me."

Trish hugged each of them, and slid into the front seat of the mini-van. "You guys take care now."

David slammed the door shut. "Remember what I said."

"Yeah, sure."

"I mean it."

Trish waved as Marge turned the van in the graveled drive. Caesar yipped beside them halfway down to the county road. Trish stared out the window.

When the van turned out onto the blacktop, Trish took in a deep breath and let it out. "Mom, I meant it about you and Patrick coming to see us run. Maybe that'll be the boost I need."

"All right. Call me with the date and times. I should have been down before now but there's been so much to do. And I hated to leave home."

"Great." Trish settled back in her seat. Another idea niggled at the corner of her mind. She chewed on her cuticle. "You been talking with the Shipsons?"

"Some, why?"

The idea burst forth like a Fourth of July rocket. "We could go to Kentucky—you and me. On Labor Day weekend. Mrs. Shipson said to come anytime. Please, Mom, please!"

"I don't know, Tee. If we come to your race—then we have to ship the horses home again—and get you ready for school—and . . ."

"We've never had a trip together, just you and me." Trish turned so she could watch her mother's face. "Please."

"Let me think about it." Marge flashed Trish a smile. "But I don't see why not."

"Yes!" Trish settled back in her seat. Who would have believed she and her mother would plan a trip together—to a horse farm, no less. Things certainly were changing.

———

Trish caught herself still humming the next morning at the Finleys when she got out of bed at the first ring of the alarm. When she looked in the mirror on the drive to the track, she saw a smile on her face.

Her "Good morning" to Adam and Carlos carried a lilt. She neatly sidestepped Gatesby when he attempted a love bite, and spent a few minutes comforting Firefly for not being ready for a morning work yet.

When she trotted Gatesby out, they entered the smaller track because morning works were about finished. Trish had left her jacket back at the office, the sun being quite warm after peeling away the early fog.

The gelding fought her all around the track. He wanted to run, and Adam had decreed a trot. Trish felt like lead weights were draped over her arms. As they rounded the far turn, the screech of brakes shattered the commuting hum on the freeway. The crash of colliding cars echoed over the track.

Gatesby whirled, and before she realized what was happening, Trish catapulted over his shoulder and thumped onto the dirt. She watched Gatesby finally take his run around the track alone.

"Stupid—good-for-nothing—" Trish called him every name she could think of. When she could breathe evenly, she got to her feet and dusted herself off.

"You okay?" One of the officials stopped to ask while

the others chased after her horse.

"Yeah, I'm fine. Thanks." Trish watched Gatesby lead the riders around the track again. Finally one grabbed a rein and pulled him to a stop.

"You want a ride back?" The man leaned forward to give her a hand up. Trish nodded and swung up behind him.

"Looks like a real bad accident out there."

"I know. And I should know better than to take my mind off my mount even a moment. My horse was asking for trouble."

"And you got it. Happens to the best of us." He dropped her at the gate where the other official held Gatesby in tow.

"Thanks." Trish took the reins and led the sweaty horse back to the stable. She spent the time explaining to him exactly how he should have behaved (in no uncertain terms).

It's your fault, Nagger leaped into the fray. *If you'd been paying better attention . . .* Trish wished she'd landed on her resident critic.

Gatesby rubbed his forehead against her shoulder. He knew better than to act up now.

"What happened?" Adam strode toward her as soon as he saw her walking. "Are you all right?"

"Yeah, I think my pride hurts worse than my posterior. There was a major crash out on the freeway. I looked over, and my friend here dumped me. I know better than that. What's the matter with me?"

"Trish, Trish . . ."

"I can't even stay on a horse for a trot around the track, let alone win anything."

"Trish!"

"What?" She finally looked up, caught by the command in his voice.

"That could've happened to anybody. It's no big deal; no one was hurt . . ."

"But they could have been. Gatesby could have been injured . . ."

"But he wasn't. Just be grateful no one was hurt." With that, Adam left her to her thoughts.

Trish drew circles in the dirt with the toe of her boot. She tried to recapture the peace of the morning by remembering how good the weekend at home had been. Instead, she felt like she was falling into the black pit again.

You had such a good time, even without your dad there, Nagger reminded her. Trish felt like a hand was clenching her heart—and twisting it. How could she be happy without her father there? How could any of them go on like they were? Why had she invited her mother to go to Kentucky with her—it should have been her dad. Her breath was coming in short gasps. Her heart pounded like Gatesby's must have after his run.

She leaned against the office wall, struggling to get her breath. The war in her head—it was too much. Her eyes filled. She grabbed her purse from the cabinet and dug for a tissue. Four white pills lay in the bottom of the tan leather envelope bag.

"They'll make you feel better." She could almost hear Richard's voice in her ear.

Anything to feel better. Trish clenched a pill in her hand and strode to the water fountain. She turned the crank with one hand and watched the water arc in the sunlight. She placed the pill on her tongue and leaned forward.

CHAPTER EIGHT

"Sorry."

The bump made her snort water. She coughed. Pill and water spewed across the gravel. Trish choked and gagged a second more.

"Really, I'm sorry."

She turned and flung her arms around the young boy beside her. "No, thank you!" She patted his cheek and beamed into his dark brown eyes. "Thank you."

Trish stepped back while the boy got a drink. He kept watching over his shoulder, as if worried what she might do next.

Trish took a drink—a long drink of plain, cold water. That had been a close call. She glanced over her shoulder. The boy walked backwards, keeping a wary eye on her.

That afternoon she brought one of Adam's horses in for a place in the first race of the program.

"I don't want to hear it," Adam ordered before she could even say a word. "That was better than I expected him to do."

"But I . . ."

He held up a hand to stop her. "No. Just be glad for a place."

Trish thought about his words on the way out to the beach. "Just be glad." Why was it so hard to be glad

91

anymore? She thought of the weekend at home. They'd laughed and had a good time. If only her father were around to enjoy it, too.

After settling all her gear on the sand at the beach, Trish drew her father's journal out first. When she read his words, she could almost hear his voice saying them to her. She opened to the first page. In bold letters, he had written: *To God be the glory. Amen. Hal Evanston.*

She traced the letters with a fingertip. That was her dad all right—giving God the glory no matter what. She flipped the pages, reading snatches here and there. He too had pleaded *why*? One page was blurred with a water spot. Had his tears fallen like hers?

She continued reading. *Even your Son cried, "My God, my God, why hast thou forsaken me?" Father, I feel so alone. The pain—knowing I brought this on myself. I did this to my family who are more dear to me than life itself. I did it. How will they ever forgive me?*

Trish buried her face in her hands. "Oh, Dad." When she could see clearly again, she returned to the same page. *But, Father, I know one thing for sure. You are in control and you love my family even more than I do. You only are worthy of praise. My Lord and my God.*

Trish shut the book. How could he do that? How?

She flipped it open again, farther back. Again, the words of praise. She flipped the pages. It was on each one. One time it was underlined and written over so the stark words leaped off the page: *I WILL PRAISE THE LORD!* Another: *GOD IS MY STRENGTH!*

Trish stuffed the book back into her bag and staggered to her feet. She ran down to the water and let the cold surf bathe her feet. Then, turning to the left, she trotted down the beach, her feet leaving deep imprints in the packed wet sand. When she reached the rocks blocking her way, she turned and started back, running until a pain pierced her side and her lungs burned for air.

She dropped back on her blanket, gasping, with sweat pouring from her face. She fished a Diet Coke out of her cooler and popped the top. As her breathing steadied and her heart rate returned to normal, Trish made a decision. She held the cool can to her cheeks for a minute longer before pulling her own journal out of the bag.

On the flyleaf she wrote, *I WILL PRAISE THE LORD!* She turned to the first blank page and began writing as fast as her pen would allow. *If my father could live a life of praise when he was dying of cancer, I will do so, too. I will give God the glory. I will ask for help. I will. Beginning right now.* She dated it and signed her name.

Then in bold, underlined, and with the letters blackened by repeated over-strokes, she wrote, *GOD IS MY STRENGTH!*

Trish flopped back on the blanket, drained as if she'd run a marathon. On the wings of the gull, the sigh of the wind, the swish of the blowing sand, she heard her song. Trish sang the words to the chorus between huffs on the upward path. She sang it again while she wrapped the journals and the eagle carefully and put them back into the backpack. She hummed the tune on the drive up the winding road.

———

"Take out paper. This is your last quiz for the quarter." The instructor stood in front of the room with a smile on his face. Was this supposed to be good news?

Trish muttered her verse as she opened her notebook.

"God is my strength. God is my strength." She threw in an "I will praise the Lord" as the teacher wrote the problems on the board.

She took a deep breath and focused on the first question.

"Just dissect each equation," Richard's voice floated in her mind. "And concentrate."

She could hear David repeating over and over. "Concentrate, Tee. Concentrate. Focus on what you're doing. You can do this." He might as well have been sitting right beside her.

When she started to panic, Trish brought her mind back with her verses. After correcting the quiz, Trish felt like shouting. She'd only missed two. A record!

The high stayed with her all the way home. She danced up the steps and through the door. Yes! She'd only missed two. Yes! She could do it!

"You look like you've got good news." Martha looked up from her needlepoint.

"I only missed two problems on the last quiz of the quarter!" Trish's feet tapped out a dance step.

"Wonderful! Oh, there's a letter here for you." Martha pointed to the hall table. "From Kentucky."

Trish danced back to the entry. She picked up the envelope. Red's handwriting sent a warm squiggle down to her middle. She slit open the envelope. The card showed a kitten hanging desperately from a branch with outstretched claws. Inside, the words "Hang in there" made Trish smile.

Dear Trish, he began. *Thanks for your card. I am now sure you didn't fall off the face of the earth. I hit the winner's circle twice yesterday. Can you believe that? Of course, two days before that I got dumped on my butt. No injuries, unless you count the ones to my pride. I think of you every day. I wish California and Kentucky weren't so far apart. Good thing prayers can cross mountains because I'm pray-ing you are better and that I'll see you again—soon. Love, Red.*

To Trish, the *soon* leaped out in big letters. *So do I,* she thought. *You're like Rhonda; you make me laugh.* She thanked Martha Finley for the mail and skipped up the stairs to her room.

———————

But all the next week, Trish felt at the mercy of the yo-yo kid. She'd be going along just fine, even remem-bering to give God the glory, and then something would trigger the sadness. It might be a word, the way someone walked, a repeat of a past event, and she'd fall down again. The pain would come crashing back, bringing tears and droopy spirits.

She forced herself to keep her mind on the horse she was riding and the others around her, but when driving the car, her mind could freewheel.

"I even cry in the shower." She tried to joke about it to Martha when she went home for lunch on Monday.

"I know. The tears catch you when you think every-thing is okay. When I lost my mother, doing dishes was hard for me. Me and the tap water, we'd flow together."

"Did they—the tears—ever go away?" Trish folded and creased her napkin with shaky fingers.

"Not completely. Sometimes, all these years later, I think of something my mother and I could have done together and the tears come. But as time passed, the crying didn't hurt as bad and didn't last as long. And the bouts were much farther apart."

"People keep telling me, time will make things easier, but . . ." Trish crumpled the napkin, then flattened it again.

"The passage of time helps, but I believe God brings the real deep-down healing."

"Mom says I need to see a doctor because I want to sleep all the time. You know anyone?" Trish made a face. "I hate to go to a doctor, especially a new one. Maybe I could wait until I go home."

Martha pushed back from the oak and glass table. She fetched a card from the file by the phone. "Here. I think you'll like her."

"Thanks, I guess."

"Something else . . . I tried to find two things I could be thankful for every day. Of course, that was after I got over being mad at God for taking my mother."

Trish felt her mouth drop open. "You were mad, too?"

"Everyone is. That's part of grieving."

Trish traced the outline of the pink flowers on her plate with the tines of her fork. "I think—" she closed her eyes to concentrate. "I think that part, being so mad all the time, is getting better."

"I think so, too."

The talk helped—for a day or two.

Talking to the doctor helped too. When Trish told her all that had gone on, the woman said, "Of course you're tired all the time. That's one way the body tries to heal itself. You need to get extra rest and eat properly."

"But that's when the nightmares come back." Trish studied the knuckles on her right hand, then looked up

at the doctor. "I see my dad as he was the—the last—"
Tears swamped her words. "The last time I saw him.
He . . ."

The doctor let her patient cry, handing over tissues
as needed. When Trish sat, calm and spent, the doctor
asked. "How did he look?"

"Like he was asleep, only I could tell he—he wasn't
there anymore."

"Did he look in pain?" Trish shook her head. "Was it
awful to look at him?"

Trish peered through her tears. "No, it wasn't bad. I
just wanted him to come back so bad . . . I want my
father back."

"I know, Trish. But death doesn't have to be a nightmare. You know he would have stayed with you if he
could, but his body couldn't handle any more."

Trish studied the doctor's kind face. "I know, but I
still miss him so."

"Yes, and that will always be. But nightmares scare
us because we see things we don't understand. Death is
a natural part of living."

"But aren't you supposed to die when you're old?"

"Usually, but life isn't always as we think it should
be, and death often comes before we're ready for it. I
could recommend a group for you if you'd like. There's
a counselor and other young people like you, who've lost
a parent or someone close to them."

Trish shook her head. "I won't be here that long."

"Okay. How about if I write a name and phone number on this pad and you call them if you want to? In the
meantime, let's give you a once over, even though I'm
almost certain there's nothing wrong with your body."

"Yeah, it's all in my head." Trish blew her nose again.

"And your heart. It takes a while for a broken heart to heal."

"I'll call you if anything shows up in the blood work," the doctor said after the tests were finished. "In the meantime, rest when you can, eat right, and think about calling that group."

"Thanks." Trish left the office feeling lighter again.

That night on the phone, when she told her mother about the doctor's suggestion, Marge said, "Groups like that do help. I go to one every Thursday."

"You do?"

Trish fell asleep that night after reading her Bible and slept through the night.

After works the next morning, Trish and Adam sat in the office munching their favorite breakfast, bagels and cream cheese.

"Hey, I like this one." Trish held up her bagel, spread with walnut-raisin-cinnamon cream cheese. "What other kind did you get?"

Adam picked up the container and read the label. "Spinach/garlic. You'll know you're an adult when you like this one."

"Hah! Carlos, which do you like best?"

"All of them. You riding this afternoon?"

Trish nodded. "Two mounts. I'm coming up in the world." She licked the cheese from her fingers. "I've been meaning to ask you guys . . . Mom and Patrick said we should keep our eyes open for a good claimer."

"How much do they want to go?" Adam crossed his feet on his desk.

"I don't know. But if I buy part of it, I'd rather have a filly."

"Is Patrick going to train for anyone else?"

"I think so. At least for the owners we had before. With David going off to school, we'll have to hire help."

"There's a gelding running on Saturday that might be one to look at." Carlos leaned against the doorframe. "I'd buy him myself if I had the money. Just coming back from a quarter crack in the off-rear hoof. Hasn't been handled right either, far as I can tell."

Trish shrugged. "So much for my idea of a filly. How much is the claim?"

"Thirteen thousand. I'll find out when he's working tomorrow."

"Okay. I'll call Mom tonight. We can look at his papers today, can't we?"

At their nods, Trish stood up. "I better get going. I'll come by after the fourth."

Mounted in the saddling paddock a couple of hours later, Trish felt the stirrings of excitement. Her butterflies must have sensed it, too, for they started their pre-race warm-ups. Trish listened carefully to the trainer's instructions. Her butterflies proceeded to aerial flits and flutters.

The gelding she rode trotted docilely beside the pony rider. The trainer had said this old boy needed waking up. Trish tightened the reins and squeezed her heels into his sides. The gelding pricked his ears and danced sideways.

Trish kept tuning him up, right into the starting gates. When the gun went off, so did the gelding. He lit out for the turn as if there were tin cans on his tail. She let him run, pacing the horses on either side. They were three across coming out of the turn. The gelding ran easily, and with two furlongs to go Trish made her move.

One swing of her whip and he stretched out. Another

and he took the lead. "Go for it, you wonderful beast!" Trish urged him on, the finish pole thundering closer. A nose crept up on her right side. Even with her boot, the shoulder, the neck.

She went to the whip and the two dueled the final strides. But it was number three to win by a nose, giving her a place.

Trish vaulted to the ground. The black clouds took up their positions on her shoulders—again.

"Good race, young lady. He ran better for you than he has for anyone. When I told you to wake him up, you did a fine job."

"Thank you. Sorry it wasn't the win." The simple words didn't begin to communicate Trish's feeling of regret. He should have won.

The black cloud hung close when Trish mounted again. The filly, entered in her first race, exhibited little to no confidence as she tentatively did what Trish asked. She tiptoed into the starting gate. The gun and the gate startled her so she broke off-balanced. It took till half the backstretch for her to gain her stride.

"Come on, baby," Trish crooned instead of yelling. The filly opened up and headed for the pack surging in front of her. She swung wide to pass the clustered horses and, coming out of the turn, seemed to realize what she was supposed to do. But too many seconds were wasted in learning and she tied for fourth.

Trish bit her lip to be polite to the trainer. He congratulated her for the fine riding job. *If you'd finished training that horse, she might have won.* Trish roped the words before they left her mouth and corralled them in her mind.

And you should have ridden her this morning so you'd

have known how to handle her, Nagger added to the shouting match already going on.

"Yeah, I know." Trish slapped her whip against her boots. If only she could go to the beach, but it was too late in the day. She had lab tonight and somehow had to find time to make up a couple of labs that she'd missed.

Or, messed up on, Nagger reminded her.

On the way to inspect the gelding, Adam and Carlos took one look at her face and refrained from commenting—on the races, the weather, or even the horse.

"I don't really like him," Trish muttered as they walked back to the barn.

"I'm not surprised," Adam answered.

Trish ignored his tone. To question him would be too much trouble. Right now, anything was too much trouble. It took all her energy to drive to the college.

At least she didn't burn the place down. But driving home, she could barely keep her eyes open.

You said you'd give God the glory, the voice in her head gloated.

"Oh, shut up!" She fell across her bed exhausted.

CHAPTER NINE

"Rhonda, over here!"

"Trish, I made it, I really made it!" Rhonda, her crop of carrot-colored hair flying as she zigzagged between the crowd, waved her hand, and jumped to see over the shoulder of a woman in front of her. "Excuse me . . . Excuse me." Finally, she dropped her bag and collapsed into Trish's arms.

A woman in a tailored business suit glared at them both. "Teenagers . . ." she muttered as she passed them.

The two girls looked at each other, at the woman's broad-shouldered back, and burst out laughing.

The giggles overwhelmed them again as they held each other at arm's length. They sank into two chairs until they could catch their breath.

"Welcome to California!" Trish tried to adopt a straight face—and failed.

"So, how much can we cram into three days?" Rhonda picked up her bag and pulled Trish to her feet.

"I thought we'd go to the beach today. I have two mounts tomorrow—Gatesby is one—and then I took Sunday off. We can shop or sightsee or . . ."

"Yes!"

"Yes what?"

"All of the above!" Rhonda dropped her bag again and

whirled Trish around in a circle. "I want a drop-dead outfit for the first day of school. Something so different, no one at home will have anything like it. Just think, we're seniors this year!"

"Excuse us . . ." An elderly couple waited for the girls to stop blocking the aisle.

"We're going shop-ping!" Rhonda flung an irresistible grin at them.

"Have fun, dear." The white-haired woman smiled back.

"We will!"

Rhonda talked non-stop all the way to Half Moon Bay and out to Redondo Beach. "Wow, this is super!" She raised up in the seat to look over the windshield. The beach curved from the space-station-looking government buildings on the north to the Strawberry Ranch promontory on the south. White frosted breakers curled onto the golden sand, rolling in from the blue-green ocean.

"No surfers. I thought California beaches had surfers."

"There are some at the jetty; that's a couple of miles up the road. We can go there if you'd rather."

"How about later?"

"Sure."

"So this is where you come all the time." Rhonda sat back down and opened the car door.

"Yep." Trish got out and went around to open the trunk. "I brought the blanket and cooler. There's no place to change if you want to put your suit on. The water's so cold here I don't really swim, so shorts are usually fine."

"Okay." Rhonda stuffed her bag into the trunk. "I'm ready."

They slid and slithered their way to the warm, dry sand, then trudged south to Trish's favorite place. Even her gull hovered nearby, circling and dipping in the hopes the girls had treats. Together they spread the blanket and plopped down.

"No wonder you like it here." Rhonda lay spread-eagle on the blanket. "There's hardly anyone else around."

"More today than usual." Trish nodded at a woman with three school-age boys playing in the waves with their black lab. A couple shared a blanket, absorbing the rays. "You want a pop?" At Rhonda's nod, Trish opened the cooler and pulled out two Diet Cokes.

As they popped the tops and poured the cold liquid down their throats, they both sighed.

"So, how are things *really* going?" Rhonda brushed her hair back from her face with one hand and tilted her pop can with the other.

"Up and down. I think I'm a yo-yo sometimes and don't know who is jerking the string."

"I'd hoped things would be better by now."

"So did I." Trish crossed her legs and pushed to a stand. "Come on, let's go walk in the water and I'll fill you in on all the gory details."

"Can we leave your stuff?"

"I always do. So far nothing's been stolen. I think the stories you hear of everything being lifted are totally exaggerated." She walked toward the waves, dragging her bare feet in the loose sand.

"Yikes! This is as cold as Washington coast water. I thought California water was warmer."

"Told you so. That's farther south. Here, you wear a wet suit or freeze."

They stayed in the shallows where the waves rolled and receded, sometimes splashing their knees but mostly just swooshing at their ankles.

"So, how's your riding coming?"

"Don't ask."

"Hey, this is me, Rhonda, your best friend, remember? To me you tell all."

Trish conceded and told her about the poor showings at the track, her difficulty with chemistry classes, how she fell asleep all the time, the pit that seemed to yawn at her feet. She told about the Finleys, how good they were to her, how she overheard some guys say she was all washed up, and how she missed Spitfire. And finally, she mentioned the journals, the song, and missing her dad. She didn't mention the pills.

"Pretty bad, huh?"

"A doctor I saw, because Mom insisted, said I maybe should join a group she knew of for kids who've had someone near to them die."

"You gonna go?"

"No. I leave for home in a couple of weeks. Things were better when I was home." Trish stopped and tossed water with one foot, staring out at the horizon.

"Bet you could find a group like that at home. I'd go with you if that would help."

"Thanks." Trish stuck her hands in the back pockets of her cut-offs. "One day I thought about walking out into the surf and not stopping, but that was quite a while ago."

"Trish, no!"

"Don't freak. I won't. My dad's journals have helped a lot. Did I tell you he wrote me a letter in the blank book he left for me? He hoped I'd start a journal, too."

Rhonda shook her head. "We haven't had much time to talk lately, if you recall. What did he say?"

"You can read it if you like. It always makes me cry. Of course, everything makes me cry nowadays."

"Remember, we used to laugh until we cried."

"Yeah, a lifetime ago." They returned to the blanket and two more cans of Coke. The wind picked up from out at sea and raised goose bumps on their arms as they sat watching the sun sink into the clouds layered on the horizon.

"Let's go," Trish said suddenly. "I know a great mini-mall with bargain stores calling our names. Tomorrow, after the races, I thought we could drive out to the Stanford Mall. It's something else."

"Stanford . . . as in Stanford University?"

"Sure. Palo Alto isn't far from here."

"You mean, like maybe we could drive around the campus? I would love to go to school there."

"Yeah, right. What independently wealthy relative is bank-rolling your education?"

"It's pretty tough, huh?"

"Uh-huh, and you have to be a near genius to get accepted there."

"So far I have a four-point average."

"Good for you. Here, which do you want to carry, the cooler or the blanket? This hill could get you in shape for a marathon."

———

They spent the hours till closing trying on tons of clothes. While the number of packages they toted grew with each store, they still hadn't found *the* outfit—for either of them.

"Tomorrow! If we can't find what we want at Stanford Mall, it hasn't been made yet." Trish slammed the trunk shut on their latest buys.

"Are the mall prices as bad out there as the school prices?"

"Don't worry about it. I'm buying."

"You idiot." Rhonda thumped Trish on the shoulder. "You can't do that. You already bought my plane ticket."

"Rhonda, think it through. I have more money than you and I can picture, so if I want to spend some on my best friend, I will. You'd do the same, now wouldn't you?"

"What did we use to say? 'All for one and one for all.' You, me, David, and Brad. Remember?"

"Yeah, back in the good old days ... before my dad ..." Trish choked on the words. She turned the ignition and her car roared to life.

"You can sleep in, you know. I'll go over for morning works, then come back for you before the race. Or, Martha said she could bring you over."

"They sure are nice, the Finleys." The two girls were sprawled on Trish's bed after visiting downstairs for a while. "I can get up with you. I haven't been at a track so early since last summer, I guess."

"Okay, but bring a book along or something. You can't go up in the jockey room with me, so you'll have quite a wait until the afternoon program starts."

"Fine, you know me. I always have a book or two along." She indicated her bag, the corners of books poking out the canvas fabric.

"Or you could stay here and catch some rays out on the deck."

"The sun doesn't shine at the track?"

"Most people don't walk around at Bay Meadows in a swimsuit, you nut."

Trish fell asleep with a smile curving her lips. Her last thought winged heavenward. Thank you, God, for Rhonda.

"Hey, I think she remembers me," Rhonda exclaimed as Firefly greeted her with a whicker in the morning.

"She should. You helped train her." Trish rubbed behind the filly's ears and down her neck. "And of course, you remember Gatesby."

"How could I forget?" Rhonda held on to the gelding's halter as she stroked his neck. "Still up to your old tricks, I hear." Gatesby twitched his upper lip to the side, as if reaching for her hand. "Oh, no you don't!"

"You never give up, do you, fella." Trish slipped the bit in his mouth and the headstall over his ears. "Now we just warm up so you can save all your energy for this afternoon." She led him out so Carlos could cinch the saddle.

Adam handed her a helmet. "Now watch him. He's primed, fit to bust."

Trish touched her whip to her helmet. "Yes, sir. He's not gonna dump me again. I still have a bruise from the last one."

"What happened?" Rhonda looked up at Trish seated on the rangy gelding.

"Ask Adam. He loves to tell tales on me." Trish nudged her mount forward. "See you soon."

Gatesby was indeed ready to run. He snorted and danced to the side, but when Trish lightly thwacked him with the whip, he jumped forward, then settled down.

Anytime he started to jig, Trish pulled him back to a flat-footed walk. About halfway around the track, she let him extend to a gentle jog, as long as he behaved. Even Gatesby realized she meant business after she thwacked him the second time.

They returned to the barn with both of them tuned up for the coming race.

Trish walked Firefly around the entire track for the first time since the filly had strained her leg. After hassling with Gatesby, the filly was pure joy.

"Come on back to the track with me," Adam said after Trish finished with a couple more horses. "I want to show you something."

Trish looked at Rhonda and shrugged. They walked with Adam out to the platform overlooking the smaller track.

"See that chestnut on the far side, the one with blinkers?"

"Sure." Trish took the binoculars he offered and studied the horse trotting nearer the freeway. "What about him?"

"Tell me what you see."

"Filly? Colt? What is it?"

"Gelding. Three-year-old."

"I don't know. He moves well, kinda leggy and rangy like Gatesby; too far to see his eyes, and with the blinkers you can't really tell about his head. Looks to be in pretty good condition. Why?"

"That's the claimer you said you didn't like."

"Oh." Trish handed back the binoculars. "Maybe we—I should look again, huh?"

"I talked to Patrick and your mother about him; faxed them the information. They said if we think so, that's good enough for them."

Trish watched the horse carefully as he galloped by them. What hadn't she liked about him? She thought back. She hadn't liked much of anything right then. *You'd have turned down Spitfire that day,* Nagger whispered in her ear.

"You really think he would pay off for us?"

"With an old pro like Patrick training him, I think you'd see some real wins with him." Adam turned back to the barns. "You want me to start the paperwork?"

Trish nodded. "I guess."

Gatesby was raring to go when Trish mounted him in the saddling paddock. He pranced and danced his way past the stands and out to the starting gates. Trish felt him quiver as the last gate slammed shut. A moment of hushed silence and they were racing. Gatesby surged from stall number four and headed for the first turn in the mile-long race. Into the backstretch, Trish held him three paces off the leader and right even with two others. Around the far turn, and the horse on their right made his move.

The jockeys went to the whip. Trish gave Gatesby more rein and crouched tighter into his neck. Gatesby lengthened out, left the one he paced behind, and passed the second-place horse. Trish swung her whip once and the gelding laid back his ears. They edged up on the front runner, each stride bringing them closer to the lead.

The other jockey whipped his horse again. Gatesby drove for the finish line. The two dueled, neck and neck.

Trish asked Gatesby for more. He gave it, and the other horse matched him. Thundering down the track, locked together, they crossed the finish line.

Trish had no idea who won. She rose in her stirrups

and let Gatesby slow of his own accord. *Photo-finish* was flashing on the scoreboard when she trotted back to the front of the winner's circle. She walked him in a tight circle, her mind pleading, *Let us win, let us win.*

Number five flashed on the scoreboard as the announcer boomed the same over the loudspeaker. Number four to place. She clamped her teeth on her bottom lip to stop the trembling. They didn't win. He should have won.

"You rode a fine race, girl." Adam held the bridle while she slipped to the ground. "Now, you have nothing to feel bad about. You—he—you both did your best, hear me?"

Trish unhooked her saddle and slung it over one arm. "Yeah, sure." She strode off to the scale.

As soon as she could get away, Trish and Rhonda walked back to the car. "See, I told you," Trish said. I can't win anymore. What do I think I'm doing out there?" She slammed the palm of her hand against the steering wheel of her car. "A *real* jockey would have brought Gatesby in first."

"Trish."

"It's not fair to a good horse . . . to put me up on him."

"Trish." Rhonda raised her voice.

"This was his last race down here and he shoulda won it."

"Trish!" Rhonda pounded her hand on the dashboard.

"What? I'm not deaf. I heard you."

"Coulda fooled me. You quit tearing yourself down like that. That race could have gone either way and you know it."

"All I know is that I didn't win." Trish drove toward

the condominium. "I need to shower and change clothes before we go."

"Go where?"

"To the Stanford Mall, remember?" Her tone cut the air like a whip.

"We don't have to go."

"No, no I want to. Maybe it'll make me feel better."

Trish tried to drive out the drummers in her head with the shower spray but it didn't help much. And when she saw another card from Red on the hall table as she left, she felt lower. The pit yawned before her.

Shopping with Rhonda seemed to drag her back from the edge. They tried on clunky jewelry, funky hats, and outrageous boots. They cruised the aisles of Saks, I. Magnin, and Macy's.

They both bought shoes at Nordstrom's.

"Look." Rhonda grabbed Trish's arm and pointed at a window across the courtyard. "That's it."

They walked into the store. Half an hour later, each was richer by one brocade vest, a long-sleeved silk shirt in hues to match the vest, a blue denim skirt, and wide belt with silver conch buckle. While their outfits matched in style, the colors fit each girl.

"Will your boots go with this?" Trish asked as they left the store.

Rhonda crinkled her face. "They should."

"Want new ones?"

"Trish, no. This is enough."

"No it isn't. Come on." When they left the boot store, they each had new boots and leather purses to match.

"Are you hungry?" Trish asked.

"More thirsty."

"Come on." They tucked their packages under the

table in a sidewalk cafe and ordered ice tea while they studied the menus.

After the waitress brought their drinks and took their orders, Rhonda leaned her elbows on the table and looked directly at her friend. "Trish, I can't believe we just did that . . . you did that."

"What?" Trish took a long swig of her drink.

"Bought all that stuff." Rhonda toyed with her straw.

"Listen, my friend. Remember all the time you spent helping David and me in the last year?"

"Yeah, but your dad paid me for that."

"He could never pay you enough. You helped keep me . . ." Trish sniffed and took another drink of tea. "You helped me feel better today, too."

Rhonda blinked a couple of times and sniffed also. "Okay. Thank you."

They both blew their noses in the paper napkins and asked for replacements when the waitress returned with their croissant sandwiches.

———

On Sunday they crammed three days' sightseeing into one. They hung from the sides of the cable car past Chinatown, up Knob Hill, then down the hills again to the turntable between Fisherman's Wharf and Ghirardelli Square.

"Come on, we have to share a sundae at Ghirardelli. Besides, there're neat shops there." Trish started up the sidewalk lined with vendors of T-shirts, sweatshirts, jewelry, and artwork of every kind. "Come on, we'll never see it all if you insist on looking at every pair of earrings here." Trish dragged Rhonda, protesting, onward.

They placed their order at the counter of the world-famous ice cream and candy shop in Ghirardelli Square, then walked through the display showing how cocoa turned from beans, that looked like coffee beans, into real chocolate.

"Creamy, dark chocolate." Rhonda drooled at the sight of the rich brown river streaming between two stones.

"Let's find a table before you faint." Trish grabbed her friend's arm. "I should have known better than to bring a chocoholic like you in here." She plunked their packages down at a round table and went up to get their order when the young man behind the counter called their number.

"I can't believe that," Rhonda whispered, her eyes as big as her mouth. The scoops of ice cream, hot fudge, and whipped cream dripped over the sides of the tulip glass and down onto the plate.

"Eat fast before it melts." Trish dug in with a long-handled spoon. "Ummmm." She let the ice cream slip down her throat and licked the fudge from the back of the spoon.

"Good thing we didn't order two."

Afterward, they laughed at the antics of the street clowns and mimes, accepting funny balloon hats from one clown. They bought San Francisco sweatshirts and watched the sun go down over the Golden Gate Bridge from the deck above the sea lions on Pier 39.

"There's another neat chocolate store here," Trish said as they turned away from the barking sea lions spread over the boat docks below.

"Oh-h." Rhonda groaned. "I'm still full from the sour-dough bread and shrimp cocktails. And our sundae."

"You don't have to eat any, just look. Everything in

the store is made of chocolate."

Rhonda bought chocolate cable cars to take home for souvenirs. She handed Trish a piece of fudge as they strolled the wooden pier.

Back home that night, they showed Martha all their purchases.

"You about bought out the town." Martha fingered the brocade stitching on the vests. "These are beautiful. You'll knock 'em dead when you walk into school wearing these outfits."

"I've never had a silk shirt before." Rhonda held her cream-colored one up in front of her.

"You think I have?" Trish hung her things in the closet. She stroked the sleeve of her flaming-rust shirt. "But doesn't it feel heavenly?"

"Did you bring an extra suitcase?" Martha asked, looking at all the things Rhonda needed to pack.

"Just this." Rhonda held up her sports bag. "And it was full when I came."

"No sweat. We'll buy you a new one in the morning." Trish yawned and went into the bathroom to brush her teeth. "Just stack the stuff on the floor so we can get in bed."

———

Rhonda lay out on the deck, sunning, when Trish returned from the track in the morning. Trish changed into her swimsuit, and after pulling up another lounger, flopped down on her stomach.

"Feeling better?" Rhonda asked.

"Better than what?"

"I can tell you're trying to be up 'cause I'm here. So,

buddy, what's buggin' you?" Rhonda turned onto her stomach.

"I haven't won a race since Belmont; I lost again Saturday, my chemistry final is coming up, and I feel like some stupid moron who can't think. That enough?"

"I guess."

"And on top of that, you're leaving today." Trish could see the pit reaching up to suck her in.

"But you said things are better than they were."

"Yeah, they are. While I check out mentally, I don't feel like checking out permanently."

"Oh, Tee, I just wish I could help somehow." Rhonda reached across the space between them and patted Trish's elbow.

"Me too."

Silence and sun lay across the deck for a time before Rhonda raised her head. "Whatever did you do with the third convertible you won?"

"It's still at the dealer. I told him I'd get back to him. I guess I will—sometime.

"Have you decided what you're going to do with it?"

"Just sell it, I guess."

"Mmmm. I liked your original idea of giving it to the youth group at church."

Trish blew out the breath she'd been holding. "Hardly."

Rhonda held up her hands. "Just a thought."

———

After she waved goodbye and Rhonda walked down the ramp to the plane, Trish felt like the pit was engulfing her again. She went through the motions of completing a make-up lab before class and listening to the instructor cover as much material as possible before the final. She couldn't decide which was worse, the dry burning behind her eyes or when they ran with tears. Either way, she ended up with a headache.

Back in her bedroom, she paced the floor, fighting to keep awake. If only she could crawl into bed and sleep, sleep away the pain, the confusion.

She forced her eyes back to the notes she'd made in class. The words turned into squiggles that danced on the page. Her gaze fell on her purse.

Richard had said the pills would help her think better. They'd give her some energy. Better than caffeine, he'd said. Just one pill; what could be wrong with taking one simple little pill? People took them all the time.

Trish picked up her purse. She dug around. Panic dried her mouth. Where were they? Finally she felt them, down at the very bottom, a baggie with the three little white pills.

She strode into the bathroom and ran a glassful of water. She put a pill on her tongue and stared at the face in the mirror.

CHAPTER TEN

There was no one to bump her this time. . . . She raised the glass to her lips and filled her mouth with water. . . . No one to tell her no.

Trish gagged and leaned over the toilet. She spit out the pill and water and gagged again.

The black pit grew before her eyes. She ran back into the bedroom and grabbed the remaining pills. The face she glimpsed in the mirror looked like it had seen a ghost. She flung the remaining pills into the toilet and flushed it.

Trish staggered back into the bedroom and sank down on the edge of the bed. Oh, to lay her head down on the pillow and forget this had ever happened. She clamped her hands to her head and rocked back and forth.

God, what do I do? Help me! The cry swirled down into the blackness engulfing her.

And He will raise you up . . .

She gulped for air.

. . . on eagle's wings . . .

Where was it coming from? *I will praise the Lord. I WILL praise the Lord. God is my strength, my very present help in times of trouble. I can do all things through Christ which strengthens me.* The verses scrolled through her mind. She could see the wall above her desk at home as if she were standing right in front of it. The wall with cards written by both her and her father. The wall of Bible verses she had memorized. *For God so loved the world, loved Trish . . .*

She grabbed the box of tissues and ripped out a handful. The tears flowed. The verses sang. Her heart settled back in her chest and resumed its steady beat. She mopped her eyes again and again. *Let not your heart be troubled . . .* That one sure fit.

A troubled heart. She sniffed and mopped.

When the tears finally dried up, she went into the bathroom and soaked a washcloth in cold water. She could almost hear it sizzle as she buried her face in it. "Thank you. Thank you." She let her shoulders droop and her head fall forward. She inhaled, a breath that went clear to her toenails. And when she released it, she felt her body relax. Another breath seemed to inhale the peace she could feel seeping into the room.

Peace floated around the room like tendrils of golden-hued clouds, kissed by the rising sun.

Trish propped her back against the headboard of the bed and her chemistry book on her lap. "Please, Father, help me read and understand what I am studying. Help me to stay awake and think clearly. I can't do this on my own. I can't seem to do much of anything right—on my own. Thank you for helping me."

Three hours of sleep wasn't enough. Trish tried rubbing the grit from her eyes but resorted to a wet washcloth instead. If only she had time for a shower—a cold one.

Remnants of the nightmare tugged at her memory. Had it been as bad as usual? She wasn't sure. If only she could wake up enough to change it like the doctor had suggested. But the end would always be the same. Her father was gone.

Dawn cracked the sky over the eastern hills as she mounted her third horse for Adam.

"Better now?" Adam patted her knee after boosting her aboard.

Trish nodded. The man could read her like a book. Did she wear her thoughts on her face like an open page or was he just a good reader?

He walked beside her out to the track. "Trot her once around, then breeze her for four furlongs. I'll be clocking you so let her go at the half-mile pole."

"Okay." Trish nudged the mare into a slow trot. The horse, long used to the routine, trotted around the outside of the track. But when Trish turned her and eased toward the rail, she perked up.

Trish could feel her mount pulling at the bit. She snapped her goggles over her eyes. She let the mare extend to an even gallop and, at the pole, let her out. The mare hit her running pace in three strides. With Trish encouraging her, the old girl flattened out, reaching for top speed. The finish pole flashed by and Trish rose in her stirrups to bring the mare back down to a gallop.

Trish and her mount hugged the rail to pass a horse galloping in front of them. Just as they pulled even, the other horse stumbled and started falling.

The mare swerved to miss the falling horse but kept to her feet, thanks to Trish's firm hands and the rail they grazed on the left. Trish's ankle took the brunt of the force.

She pulled the mare to a walk and glanced back to check on the other horse. He was limping off the track. The jockey shrugged an apology.

Trish rubbed her ankle through her boot. What a stupid thing to have happen. When would she learn to pay better attention? She checked the mare's shoulder. Part of her hide was burned bare. But she wasn't limping, seemed no worse for the near miss.

"You're okay?" Adam asked when he met her at the exit.

"Yeah, but . . ."

"I don't want to hear it." He raised his hands. "You did a good job in a tight situation and everyone came out all right."

"But . . ."

"Trish, you can't take responsibility for the whole world. Accidents happen; that's life." He examined the graze on the mare's shoulder.

"I feel like I'm an accident waiting to happen."

Adam glared up at her. He shook his head and strode off to the barns.

At the barns he said, "You might want to thank God you weren't hurt. I do." He boosted her up on Gatesby. "Give him a couple of laps nice and easy."

Trish finished her morning rides without much feeling. She felt guilty that Adam had to scold her like he did. She dragged her feet into the office and sat down on the edge of her chair. "Adam . . ." She had to clear her throat. "I—I'm sorry. I just want to be the best, or even good again, and everything seems to go against that." She looked up to see him nodding at her. "I'm up when everything's okay and down when it isn't."

"I've noticed. But you've got to take it as it comes and just do the best you can."

"My father kept on praising the Lord all through his cancer. I want to do that, too, but it doesn't come easy for me."

"Your dad was a lot older than you, Trish. Learning to thank God for everything takes time and practice. It's a lot like a mother teaching her child to say thank you. She has to remind him over and over—and over. God isn't going to smack you because you forget sometimes. He loves you too much."

"I smack myself often enough."

"And is it doing any good?"

Trish shrugged. "Maybe one of these days I'll remember."

"And in the meantime, you feel terrible."

Trish leaned back in her chair. "How come you got so smart?"

"See this white hair?" Adam pointed to the fringe around his balding head. "I earned every one of them—mostly the hard way."

———

That night when Trish returned from class, in which she'd stayed alert for a change, Martha told her that David had called.

"Thanks." Trish ran up the stairs and dumped her stuff on the floor by the bed. She dialed the number, then pulled off her boots while it rang.

Marge answered. "Good evening, Runnin' On Farm."

"Hi, Mom, it's me."

"Hi, Tee. We're getting him all packed."

"What do you mean?"

"David's leaving for Tucson tomorrow so he has time to stop and see you. Martha said they had plenty of room for him there. You'll see him some time late in the day."

"Whew, you guys don't waste any time, do you?"

"Not much." There was an awkward silence.

"Mom, are you okay?"

Trish heard a faint sniff. "I will be. It's just that this house will be awfully empty till you come home."

"Why don't you come with him?" Trish lay back on her pillows.

"I wish I could, but I've still too much to do with all the paperwork and stuff. I'm not even sure I can make it down to watch you race."

"M-o-m!"

"I know. But even though your father had his will in order and a lot of other stuff, there's still too much to do."

Trish gripped the phone till her knuckles whitened. "You have to come, Mom. I'm counting on you to help me win."

"No, Trish. You count on God and yourself for that, not me. Is there anything you want David to bring?"

"Just you."

"Rhonda came over and showed me what you bought. Her new outfit is beautiful."

"Isn't it? I have one, too. Oh, I almost forgot, we've started the paperwork on the claimer. He looks good. I wanted a filly but Carlos found this gelding. He said he'd buy it himself if he had the money."

"Good. The mare and filly come tomorrow. Sure will be busy when you're all home again."

"Well, I gotta get to sleep. See you in a couple of days."

"Trish. . . . Good-night, Tee."

So David would arrive tomorrow. Would he want to

go sightseeing too? Trish brought out her journal, propped herself up against the headboard, and began writing. She managed only two sentences before her eyes closed. The book thumping to the floor woke her enough to turn out the light and set the alarm.

"Okay, just walk her around the short track nice and easy. The swelling is gone, and if it stays down she should be okay for Sunday." Adam stroked Firefly's shoulder after boosting Trish into the saddle. "We'll need to clock her day after tomorrow, so we're cutting it pretty close."

"I'd rather scratch her than take a chance on a long-term injury." Trish smoothed a stubborn strand of the filly's mane to the right side.

"I agree, but this is the last good race for her this season and I hate to miss it unless we're forced to." He stepped back. "Have a good one."

Trish brought Diego's horse in for a show that afternoon. The horse that won ran all the others right into the ground and then left them lengths behind. Even Trish couldn't fault herself for not winning that one.

"You have nothing to say?" Adam cocked one eyebrow at her.

"Yeah, you think they want to sell that horse?" Trish looked over at the winner's circle where the colt, jockey, and entourage posed for pictures. "He was moving."

Trish lost the next one. Ended up next to last. The horse broke badly, swung wide on the turns, and ran out of steam down the stretch.

"I rode better than that as an apprentice," she muttered, following the other jockeys back to the jockey room.

She gathered up her gear and headed around the track to the barn. Maybe David would get here before she had to leave for school. But probably not. She checked her watch. She needed to go early to finish making up two more labs. At least the next day was Friday, and she had no school. Richard had canceled their last tutoring session. Maybe she could get David to coach her.

When she got in her car, her gaze automatically fell on the Post-it note on her dashboard. She'd written it as a reminder. Big letters. PTL. Praise the Lord. Sure, praise the Lord for losing a race. How about for riding a dud of a horse? It would be easy to praise the Lord if she owned the horse who won the first race.

She could thank Him that no one got hurt today. And that David was coming. There, those were her two things for the day. "And please help me finish these experiments fast. And right."

The wind felt wonderful in her hair and even the traffic moved smoothly as she drove to school.

When she got home that night, David sat in the living room visiting with the Finleys.

"You made it okay." Trish crossed the room to give her brother a hug. Strange, they never used to hug, but now it seemed natural—and necessary.

"That's a *long* drive." David rubbed the small of his back with doubled fists.

"That's why I like flying."

"There's ice tea in the fridge if you want," Martha said.

When Trish returned from the kitchen, she smacked her lips. "This is really good. You did something new."

"Added a bag of mint tea to the regular sun tea."

"I like it."

"What's sun tea?" David asked. He took another swallow from his sweating glass.

"You put the tea bags in cold water in a jug and set it out in the sun for the day."

"One of the good things about California sun." Trish chose to sit on the floor between David and the Finleys. "But the oranges alone are worth living here."

"There are some of those on the kitchen table, if you like." Martha turned to David. "Trish found out that oranges that never saw the light of a cooler are a whole different fruit."

"Like, are they ever. 'Course you'll have them in Arizona too." She took another swallow of tea. "Still, I wish you weren't going."

"You want me around to do your chemistry." He patted her on the head.

"You want to? I just happen to have some here." Trish leaned forward like she was going to get it right then.

"No, no, baby sister, you do your own homework."

"Rats." Trish finished her tea and checked the grandfather clock on the far wall. "Speaking of which, I need to go do some and hit the sack. We working people have to get up early."

"Call me when you get up. I'll be ready when you are." David leaned back on the sofa. He covered a yawn with his hand. "If you think driving down here in one day isn't work, you're crazier than I thought."

"Thank you." Trish smiled at the Finleys and rolled her eyes.

They both smiled at her antics. " 'Night, Trish."

Having David at the barns in the morning felt like old home week. When he boosted her into the saddle on Gatesby, he stood by her knee, smiling up at her.

Trish caught the flick of Gatesby's ears. Before she could do any more than open her mouth, the gelding clamped a bit of David's shirt in his teeth and yanked.

"Ouch." Gatesby obviously got more than cloth. "You idiot horse." David rubbed his upper arm. "Why we keep you around . . ." He glared up at Trish who collapsed on Gatesby's neck with laughter.

"You should s-s-see your f-face." She broke up again.

Adam and Carlos tried for all their worth to keep straight faces but Trish's laughter tickled them into joining. Trish tried to straighten up but when she looked over their heads, Juan was leaning against the barn, his shoulders shaking, his hands clasped over his mouth.

"Go ahead. All of you. Laugh it up." David clamped a hand on the reins right under Gatesby's chin and raised the other hand as if to strike. Gatesby lifted his head away and rolled his eyes. He knew how to play the game.

"It's so good to be the butt of the joke my first morning . . ."

"The bite." Trish cracked up again at her own cleverness.

"Huh?"

"Not the butt, the bite of the joke." She spoke slowly as though he didn't understand the language.

David made as if to grab her, but when he dropped the reins, Gatesby reached around and David grabbed the reins again.

"Hah, think I'll go work off some of his energy. When we get back, maybe David'll be in a better mood," Trish said for Gatesby's benefit.

"Give her a real ride, you old nag," David muttered to the horse. Gatesby tossed his head as much as the hand on his reins would allow.

Trish heard herself humming as they trotted out on the track. That *had* been fun. She stroked Gatesby's neck and patted his shoulder. "We should put you in a circus act," she told him. "Gatesby, the fastest-running clown on planet earth." Her horse jigged sideways. He seemed to enjoy the fun as much as she did.

But the fun in the morning had no bearing on the racing in the afternoon. Trish had two mounts and neither one of them made it into the money. The first one quit running in the stretch and no amount of the whip made any difference.

Trish hated to use her whip at all, let alone enough to get the horse to try harder. He just didn't have it in him.

The second one, in the third, kept pulling away from any horse that came up on his right side. And since they had the rail, that meant every horse in the field. "You might want to put blinkers on him," she mentioned to the trainer after dismounting. "Is he that shy all the time?"

"Nah, only since he took a bad bump. You're probably right." The trainer led the horse away.

Trish couldn't believe she'd offered her opinion. Only disgust had made her do it. She tried not to yell at herself, but discouragement won out. By the time she got back to the barn, she was down again.

"You want to watch the rest of the program or go to the beach?" she offered David the choice.

"The beach." He turned to Adam. "Unless we should go see that gelding now."

"Tomorrow will be fine. You two have a good time."

She drove all the way without a word. She could feel David glancing at her, waiting for a response to his comments, but she focused only on the road. She parked in her usual place, with the Pacific stretching before them. A fishing boat, dark against the gray swells, chugged north to the man-made harbor.

"So this is where you've been coming. I can see why."

"David, I'm thinking of quitting racing." There, the words were out.

CHAPTER ELEVEN

"That's the stupidest idea I ever heard."

"You saw that race. It was typical, just the way my season is going."

"Trish, every athlete, every jockey, has a down time."

"I hardly get any mounts, other than ours and Adam's."

"There are more jockeys here; the track is bigger, and so is the money. Besides that, you're not the darling here you were at home."

"I'm not a winner here either." She clamped her lips shut, then turned her head. "So you're saying my wins were because of Dad and Spitfire?"

"No, that's not what I meant. Quit twisting my words around."

"So?" She crossed her arms across her chest.

"So what?" David looked at her, confusion written all over his face.

"So, what did you mean—about me being the darling at home."

"Well." David clicked his teeth together and pursed his lips. "At home you were known before you apprenticed. Everyone liked you, and Dad had both a good name and lots of friends. And then, you had that gift . . ."

"*Had* is the right word."

"Shut up and let me finish this. You have a gift of understanding horses and getting them to perform at their best for you."

"Had, David, *had*. It's not happening anymore." Trish twisted to open her car door.

David grabbed her arm. "No. Let's get this out in the open and talk about it." As she started to pull away, he tightened his hold. "Now. You want to make Dad a liar?"

"That's a low blow if I ever heard one."

"He believed in you. I believe in you, and so does Mom. You've lost your confidence, that's all."

"David, I have tried. I do everything I can and still nothing works out right. Maybe I can come back to racing later, but for now, if I don't win a race, especially the one with Firefly before I have to leave for home, I'm quitting." She shoved open her door. "You coming down to the beach or not?"

She grabbed her bag, cooler, and blanket out of the trunk and headed for the trail.

David took the cooler from her as soon as he caught up. He followed her down the trail and out to her favorite spot.

Trish dumped the gear, removed her shoes, and scuffed through the dry, loose sand down to the wet where foamy waves scalloped an edge. She hunched her shoulders against both the inward and outward chill and watched the waves curl around her feet. The sand being sucked away from under her felt about as secure as the world she'd been living in lately.

"I can see why you like it here." David stopped beside her.

Trish raised her face to the sun. "Dad wrote about peace in his journal, and this is the place where I seem to find it best."

"Mom said she gave you his journal and the carved eagle."

"Yeah." Trish turned and started walking in the ankle-deep water. "Don't you miss him so much you want to—to . . ." She kept her gaze on the foamy water curling about her feet.

"To scream? To cry? Bash my hand against a wall?" David snorted. "Sure I have. I've done it all. And then I felt better—for a while." He turned his fist over so she could see a fading scar line. "That's what I got for it." He traced the line with a fingertip. "But you have to go on, Tee. Dad would want that."

"Have you read his journal?"

"No." David shook his head. "You had it down here."

"It's back on the blanket in my bag." She turned and started back. "Come on. We have a little bit of time before I have to leave. Chemistry calls, you know."

Back at the blanket, Trish pulled the leather-covered journal with the cross tooled on the front from her bag and handed it to her brother. "Here." She then lifted two sodas from the cooler and gave him one of those too.

While he paged through their father's journal, she wrote in her own.

After a few pages, David pushed himself to his feet. "I'll be back."

She could hear his voice choking up. But David, being David, didn't like others to see him cry. Arms wrapped around her raised knees and chin on one, she watched him walk toward the surf.

Maybe not winning is God's way of telling me to get out of racing, she wrote in her journal, as David fought his private battle on the water's edge. *While I can't see quitting forever, maybe I'm supposed to spend all my time being a senior this year, getting the good grades Mom was after me for all last year. Dad, I sure wish you were here to give me your good advice. I have said I will praise the Lord, but that's so hard when things aren't going the way you want them to.* When she rubbed the moisture from her eyes, she rubbed sand into them. Now her nose really dripped.

She tucked the journal away and rummaged for a tissue. She blew, blinked, and lying back, kept her eyes closed to let the tearing wash away the grit. She heard David's scuffling feet and then felt him drop to the blanket beside her.

"You okay?" he asked.

"Just some sand in my eyes. How about you?"

"I'll live." He tapped her arm with the corner of the journal. "I have something to ask you."

"Okay." She shielded her eyes with her arm.

"Will you please think this idea of yours through? Don't make any decisions about what you will or won't do until you talk with Mom."

"David."

"No, listen to me. You've seen how Mom is working with the babies and taking an active part in the farm. She thinks Dad would want it that way."

"David, she's the one who didn't want me to race, remember? The track was too dangerous for her little girl. . . . Maybe she'll be happy if I quit."

"All I'm asking is that you keep an open mind."

"Look who's talking. Do you think you can just tell me what to do?" She sat up and turned to him.

"I'm not telling you what to do—I'm asking." David spoke softly, gently. "I'm just asking."

Trish glared at him, trying to stare him down. But the look on his face forced her to swallow her words. "All right," she whispered. She put the books back in their bag and the empty cans in the cooler. "We better get going. I have a final on Monday."

The instructor spent the class time reviewing for the final. Trish listened with total attention and took careful notes so she'd know what best to review. For a change she didn't feel like falling asleep. Maybe it was an adrenaline high clicking in early. At least she didn't have any mounts the next day, and could spend the afternoon studying.

"Here." She handed David the Periodic Table of elements and their symbols when she got back to the car after class. "You can quiz me on them on the way home." She turned the key in the ignition. "Did you eat already?"

"Yeah. I called Mom, too."

"Wonderful."

"How'd your class go?"

Trish only shrugged. When she realized David couldn't see her response in the dark car, she said, "The teacher spent the time reviewing. The final is on Monday. Right now I just want to get it over with. If I never see another chemistry book, it'll be too soon." She turned the car into the parking lot of a take-out Chinese restaurant. "You want anything more?"

"You know I can always eat Chinese. Just get plenty and I'll eat part of yours."

Trish muttered under her breath and got out of the car. She placed the order and paced the room. *What'd he have to call home about; get Mom all worried before she needs to be? Not that she needs to worry about this, any-*

way. After all, racing or not is my decision.

"Your order is ready." The soft-spoken woman behind the counter smiled as she placed the styrofoam containers on the stainless steel surface.

"Thanks." Trish paid and walked out. *Runnin' On Farm could hire jockeys just like the other owners did. Couldn't they?*

If they could, why did the thought of someone else riding her horses give her a pain in the heart region? Would this be one part of her father's dream that fell apart?

She handed the containers in to David. As she plopped onto the seat, she spoke through gritted teeth. "You didn't have to tell Mom." They ate their dinner in silence.

———

Trish had just gotten to her room back at the Finleys' when the phone rang.

"It's for you, Trish," Martha called up the stairs.

Trish picked up the receiver. "Hello." At the sound of her mother's voice, she sat down on the bed. "Hi, Mom."

"My flight comes in at 7:00 P.M. on Saturday. Can you pick me up?"

"Sure." Trish felt her heart beat faster. Her mother was coming to see the race!

"I thought we'd go out for dinner, so think of someplace nice."

"Okay."

"So how are you doing?" Her mother's gentle question ignited the burning in Trish's eyes.

"Ummm." Trish looked up through her bangs. "I guess David told you what I've decided. And the cruddy way I rode today—I don't know. Sometimes it all seems more than I can handle."

"Ah, Tee, that's the point. You don't have to handle it, at least not all by yourself."

"Yeah, I know, but the doin' is the hard part." Trish sniffed. "Mom, I just can't stand losing all the time."

"Well, we'll talk more when I get there. The gelding runs Saturday?"

"Right. In the fifth race. I have a mount in the fourth."

"Give it all you've got. I'll see you Saturday night."

Trish tried studying for a while, but when her eyes kept drifting closed, she got up and went downstairs. David lay on the sofa watching television, with Martha working her needlepoint under the lamp. Adam had already gone to bed. Trish wished she could.

"How about helping me for a while?" She poked a finger into David's shoulder. "You don't need to see the end of this program anyhow."

He turned into a sitting position. "Didn't your mother ever teach you to say please?"

"She tried, brother dear, she tried. Come on, David, please. I can't stay awake, and you explain this stuff so it makes sense."

"Oh, all right." He rose to his feet. "Good-night, Martha. Thanks for the pie."

"Pie? You ate Chinese just before we got home!"

"Have to keep up my strength." He followed her up the stairs.

"Let's go through this thing first." She handed him a copy of the Periodic Table. "Give me the element and I'll give you the symbol."

"Iron."

"Capitol F, small e."

"Aluminum."

"Capitol A, small l." They continued on through the entire table, with David asking for weights and definitions at times.

Trish paced around the room, her brow furrowed in concentration.

"I'd say you have those down pretty good. How about a list of terms."

She handed him a sheaf of papers stapled together.

"Okay." He glanced down the page. "Stoichiometry."

Trish groaned. "The determination of the atomic weights of elements, the proportions in which they combine and . . ." She scrunched up her face. "And . . ." She gave David a pleading look.

" . . . and the weight relations in any chemical reactions."

Trish repeated the entire definition twice more. "Next."

"Avogadro's Law."

"Oh, I hate this one. Avogadro's Law is the theory that equal volumes of all gases . . ." She shook her head and started again. "Something about molecules and weights."

"Come on Trish, think."

"Avogadro's Law: equal volumes of all gases under identical conditions of temperature and pressures contain equal numbers of molecules."

"Yes!"

When Trish fell into bed an hour later, her head was full and her heart running over. If only she'd had David around all summer.

Friday morning fog gave David a taste of summer on the San Francisco Peninsula. "I'm freezing," he said as he huddled into his jacket. "Turn on the heat."

"I don't suppose you want the top down."

He gave her a dirty look. "The sun's not even up yet."

"You could have stayed at home in bed."

"And miss this? You outta your mind?"

Everyone seemed in good humor that morning, even Gatesby. He galloped the track in an even gait, not pulling against the bit more than once or twice. Trish patted his neck as she came through the exit.

"What a good fella. I was beginning to think you had it in for me." He shook his head and walked back to the barn. He didn't even shy when another horse dumped its rider and tore off down the road.

After dismounting, Trish stood right in front of the horse, took both sides of the snaffle bit in her hands, and looked him straight on. "You up to no good or don't you feel all right?"

Gatesby blew at her and tried to rub his forehead on her chest.

"Watch him, Juan. He's behaving himself."

Firefly trotted the track like the perfect lady she was. While Trish concentrated, to detect any limping on that foreleg, the filly trotted on with a strong, even beat. Trish felt a load release from her shoulders. She wasn't aware she'd been worrying about the filly.

But you said you'd quit if she doesn't win, Nagger whispered. *Your dad always said winners never quit and quitters never win. That'll make you a quitter.*

As the sun burned away the fog, Trish felt her own black cloud rolling in. *Do I really want to quit? Maybe I could call it taking a break. What's the word—a sabbatical? One year off.*

She worked the rest of the Finley string with the argument jumping back into her mind every time she dismounted.

"You sure got awful quiet," David said as he boosted her up for the last time. "You all right?"

Trish shook her head. "No, but I will be." *One of these days—or years.*

If you quit, it'll be like starting all over when you go back, Nagger threw in.

"Give it a rest!" Trish gritted her teeth. Her horse flicked his ears back and forth and broke his even gait. "No, no, not you, easy now." The animal relaxed again at Trish's soothing voice.

After works, Trish joined David, Carlos, and Adam in the office. The box of bagels and two kinds of cream cheese lay open on the desk.

Trish unfolded her chair and, after smearing spinach and garlic cream cheese on a sesame-seed bagel, sat down. She crossed one ankle over her other knee to help form a table.

"Well, what do you think of bagels?" she asked David who had his mouth full.

"He hates them; he's only on his fourth half." Adam pushed the box closer to David.

David swallowed, and after a sip of coffee, could talk. "Who's counting?"

Trish concentrated on her breakfast. Biting a bagel just the right way took plenty of thought and planning. She tried to ignore the voices in her head. She tried to ignore the voices of the men in the office. She tried to ignore the pain in her heart. She failed on all counts.

You said you'd praise the Lord, too. Remember? She jumped to her feet and threw the uneaten third of her bagel in the trash. She left the office without a word.

David found her a while later, sitting in her car, chemistry book propped against the steering wheel, sound asleep. "Trish." He shook her shoulder. "Trish, come on. Wake up."

Trish stretched her neck and rotated her head from shoulder to shoulder. She yawned fit to bust her jaw. When she blinked her eyes for the fourth time, they finally focused. "What do you want?" Her voice came out flat and dark, just like her feelings.

"You said you wanted to come along when we went to see the gelding."

"The gelding?" While her eyes might have been functioning, her brain stayed stuck in the sleep mode.

"The claimer. We have to make a decision." His voice came across so big-brother patient she nearly gagged.

Instead she yawned. This time she heard it crack.

"Well, if you're not interested, we'll go without you. But since you'll be the one training and racing him, I'd think you'd like to be there."

"I might not be the one racing him, you know."

"Ah, Trish. I don't want to hear any more about your quitting."

Trish pushed open her car door. Going with them was better than staying alone.

"I like him," David whispered in Trish's ear as they watched a woman walk the gelding around in the deep sand circle to cool him down.

"I'd rather have a filly."

"Geldings usually make more money in the long run."

"He seems even tempered. We've watched him galloping. And the stats don't lie." Trish turned back with the others.

"Why do you think he hasn't done better?" David asked as they walked back to their own office.

"He's coming back from a quarter crack on the off rear that ended his two-year-old season. I think he's a late bloomer too. He still hasn't finished growing and the owner got too ambitious in the races they entered him in. A lot of things can happen, you know." Adam seemed to be thinking out loud.

"He'll do good this year," Carlos added.

Yeah, if we get him, Trish kicked a rock ahead of her. *The way things are going, I'll probably jinx that too.*

"So you want to do it?" Adam sat back down at his desk.

David looked over at Trish. At her nod, he dug his billfold out of his back pocket and took out a check. "Mom signed this. We just have to fill in the amount."

Trish left for the jockey room. She was riding in the first race.

"How's it going?" Mandy asked as Trish walked into the locker-lined room. The wall-mounted television was on, as usual, showing past races until the day's program started.

Trish shrugged. "Still up and down, I guess. I got to go home for a few days and that helped. And then my best friend came down to shop and sightsee. Now, that was fun."

"Good. How's the racing?"

"No wins."

"Me, either. I think some of those big guys got a scam going. They just take turns, if ya know what I mean." Mandy leaned back in her chair. " 'Course, now, if I won once in a while, I probably wouldn't feel this way."

"How long you been racing?"

"Four years. Started out on the fair circuit and last year moved up to the big time at Bay Meadows. I'll try my luck at Golden Gate Fields this year too."

"You ever think of quitting?"

"You kidding? About every time I get tossed. One time I was laid up for a month; thought about it lots then. But I make a decent living and I'm doing what I like best." She took a brush out of her bag and started brushing her hair. "Besides, I don't have training for anything else."

"Did you go to college?"

Mandy shook her head. "College? Honey, I never made it through high school. Finally went back and got my GED. I wasn't kidding when I said I went downhill for a time. A hard time."

She turned and leaned her hip against the counter. "You hang in there, kid." She waved her hairbrush for emphasis. "You've been at the top. You'll get there again."

"Wish I could be so sure."

And Trish felt even more unsure after the first race. She and her mount started out well. The trainer said the colt liked to be in front so Trish got him out and kept him there. But the pace was fast and the colt gave up when another horse caught up with him.

While the trainer was happy with a show, Trish wasn't. "You did a fine job with him," the young man said. He led his horse away and Trish followed the other jockeys back under the stands and out to the jockey rooms. At least now she could head for the beach.

When David suggested driving into San Francisco, Trish shook her head. "I've gotta study. I was hoping you'd help me again. We could go to the beach." She smacked herself on the forehead. "Ah, no. I've got one more lab to make up. This afternoon's it. You could help me do my lab!"

"Right. Think I'll go into the city while you're at school. I'll help you again tonight when I get back."

"Oh, David." The cloud that hid her sun looked like rain.

CHAPTER TWELVE

Who screamed?

Trish blinked. She'd been sound asleep, but someone had screamed. She listened, every nerve ending taut. Was it someone in the house?

Nothing. She cleared her throat; it was hot and raw. Was it she who had screamed? When she thought about it, the screaming had been going on for a long time—or so it seemed.

She swallowed again. Water ... a glass of water would help. She raised her head and checked out the corners of the room, all the places she could see, anyway, in the light that filtered through the eucalyptus branches outside the deck.

The glow from the streetlights flickered. It must be blowing out there. Had the scream come from outside?

For a moment she wished she had closed the drapes. But there was nothing to be seen. She sat up and swung her feet to the floor. It must have been her. Had she screamed out loud? Had anyone heard her?

Surely they would come if they had. She tiptoed into the bathroom and filled a glass with water. After the first few swallows she could slow down and sip it.

She rubbed her throat. It hurt.

When she crawled back in bed, she was afraid to close

her eyes. It *had* been a dream. She had been screaming in the dream, but about what?

When she closed her eyes to remember, the scene flashed right back. Spitfire ran away from her. The more she called him, the faster he ran away. All the other horses, too. Firefly, Gatesby, Sarah's Pride, even Miss Tee and Double Diamond. All of them were running away.

She caught her breath. Dan'l, old gray Dan'l. She wanted to call to him but he was running after the others.

N-o-o! She sat bolt upright in bed. Tears streamed down her face. She turned on the light and reached for a tissue. What did it all mean?

When her heart finally resumed its normal beat, she lay back down. A long time ago she'd learned to say the name of Jesus over and over when she had a nightmare. "Jesus. Jesus. Jesus." She let her eyes drift closed. *Jesus, Jesus, Jesus.* She could feel her muscles relax. First in her neck and shoulders, then down her arms. She inhaled and held the breath. *Jesus, Jesus, Jesus.* When she let the breath out, she felt like she was sinking into the mattress.

Thank you, Father. I was so scared. Thank you for being right here with me. Amen.

Trish struggled up out of sleep again, but this time she knew the sound. Her alarm. She reached over and hit the snooze button.

She still felt like a field of fourteen thoroughbreds had used her body for a track when the alarm buzzed again. If she didn't get going now, she wouldn't get a shower, and if she didn't get a shower, she wouldn't make it to the track. She dragged her loudly protesting body out of bed and, after turning on the shower, stood under the pounding water until she could think.

What had the dream meant? In the Bible God used dreams to tell people things. Was He doing that now with her?

She thought back to the night before. David had helped her with her chemistry again. She'd fallen asleep asking God to help her make a decision. That was it. To quit or not to quit.

Her head ached. Along with most of the rest of her body.

She didn't feel a whole lot better by the time she arrived at the track but at least she was moving.

Dense fog muffled the morning sounds of the track. The cold mist only added to Trish's feeling of confusion.

"Let's wait a bit before we take the first one out," Adam said when she joined him and David at the stalls.

"Yeah, I love this sunny California," David said, shivering beside them. He'd brought his own car today in case he decided to do something different. "This is colder than winter at home."

"If we were across the bay, on the other side of the hills, there'd be no fog at all." Adam stuck his hands in his pockets. "Clear as a bell with the sun pinking the sky behind Mt. Diablo."

"You're kidding. Let's go there."

"No racetrack out there either." Trish tucked her chin down into her jacket collar.

"Coffee's hot. Come on." Adam led the way back to the office.

Trish accepted a mug and wrapped both her hands around it. While she didn't much care for coffee, it was good for warming hands. She added a spoonful of sugar and two of mocha-flavored creamer. The closer it came to hot chocolate, the better she liked it.

But the hot drink didn't help much out on the track. Dawn lightened the sky so that the fog floated more dingy white than gray. The jingle of gear, people's voices, and horses snorting still sounded hollow.

The wind sneaked around Trish's neck and up her cuffs, any place it could get in to chill her body. She poured herself a second cup of coffee between mounts. And this was August.

But by the time they were finished, the sun shone bright and the track slipped back into its usual cheery morning atmosphere. All except for Trish. She listened to the others discuss the training schedule and how the horses had done.

Adam and Carlos debated the relative merits of one race over another for one of the horses. David cleaned up the last of the bagels.

Trish was just leaving to go to the car to pick up her chemistry books when her agent called. Adam handed her the phone.

"I wanted to make sure you heard that the horse you were riding this afternoon was scratched," he said.

"Great." Trish couldn't keep the disgust out of her voice.

"Sorry. Talk to you later."

Trish hung up the phone, and at the question on David's face, told him what had happened.

"I could spend the afternoon at the beach if we didn't have that gelding running."

"You don't have to stay."

"Or we could go into San Francisco."

"You have to study. Remember?"

"Yeah, I know. You want to help me?"

"For a while. Then I need to go shopping. You and Rhonda aren't the only ones who need school clothes."

"You'll live in shorts most of the year. I heard it can get pretty hot there." Trish got herself a bottle of water out of the fridge. "You want to study here or at the condo?"

That afternoon Trish returned to the track in time for the fifth race. She walked over to the grandstands with Adam and David, where they all leaned on the rail.

The sun beat down hot on their heads and shoulders.

"Hard to believe the chill of the fog this morning, and hot like this now," David commented after wiping the sweat off his face for the second time.

"The paper said it was 115 in Phoenix yesterday." Adam wiped his forehead, too.

David groaned. "And Tucson is farther south. Thank God for air conditioning."

Trish listened to their conversation with only half an ear. When the bugle called for parade to post, she watched for number four. Gimmeyourheart trotted out on the track.

"I hate his name," she muttered as the gelding crossed in front of them.

"You don't have to like it. They call him Sam for short," David reminded her. "Just hope he wins so we start recouping our investment."

"If you want him to win, I better leave."

"Trish." David poked her with his elbow.

Trish gave him an I-told-you-so look when Gimmeyourheart came in sixth. "Well, Carlos, I sure hope you're right about what that beast can become. Looks to me like he needs a long vacation." *Kinda like me.* The thought galloped through her mind.

"You wait." Carlos turned from the rail with the rest of them. "When you ride him tomorrow, you'll see what I'm talking about."

Trish could see the fog rolling over the tops of the coastal hills as they left the track. The fog was coming back over the land and into her heart.

You better get a smile on your face before your mother sees you, Nagger whispered. Trish slammed the door on her mind at the same time she slammed the door of her car.

She felt the good old tears congregating as soon as she saw her mother's face in the crowd. And when Marge's eyes held the same telltale sheen, Trish gave up. They held each other close and then wiped their eyes at the same time.

"Come on, you two crybabies. I'm starved." David took his mother's bag and nodded toward the exit.

But when Trish looked up at him, she caught him blinking, too.

"You look all grown up in that outfit," Marge said as they crossed the skywalk to the short-term parking lot. "It's beautiful."

"Thanks." Trish glanced down at the rust silk blouse. "I love the feel of silk. Now I know why people rave about it all the time."

"Yeah, but the dry-cleaning bills are atrocious."

"No, this is washable. The tag says so. Rhonda and I wouldn't have gotten them otherwise. You should stay long enough so we can go shopping."

Marge looked to David walking beside her. "Is this *our* Trish, or did you bring a substitute?"

"Mother." Trish squeezed her mom's arm. "Even I can grow up. And besides, the Stanford Mall is something else."

Trish pointed out landmarks as they drove to a restaurant high on the hill overlooking the entire bay. So far the clouds remained to the west so they enjoyed the lights coming on around the bay. The San Mateo bridge arched high on the west side and then down to water level, crossing the bay like a belt with a fancy buckle.

"Okay, what's happening?" Marge asked after they'd enjoyed their dinner and conversation.

"Trish still says if she loses tomorrow, she's quitting."

"Thank you, David." She wanted to kick him in the shins.

"Want to talk about it?" Marge asked gently.

Trish shook her head but the words came anyway. "I just can't stand losing all the time. I've been wondering if this is God's way of telling me to quit; maybe only a year, but for now. I hate the word quit. I could think of it as time off."

"I've been praying about this, too," Marge patted Trish's hand. "I remember your dad saying how he always felt you had a gift for animals, especially horses. He really believed that you had all the attributes of a top-notch jockey. Sometimes I thought it was just a dream of his, but when you did so well I began to believe him." She traced around the top of her water glass. "And now I believe you are a good jockey going through a terrible time. But more than a jockey, you are my daughter. And you are becoming an adult." She reached out to clasp Trish's hand. "All I know for certain is that that will never change. You must make the decision. I won't make it for you. But whatever you decide, we'll live with it."

"All these races that I've prayed to win, and now what?"

"Would you trade a minute of it?" When Trish shook her head, Marge smiled. "How about we share a dessert?" The waiter returned to fill the coffee cups and Trish's ice tea. At their nods, she asked the waiter to bring the dessert tray.

"Let's get two," David said when he saw the fancy desserts.

They settled on a tart with raspberries and kiwi fruit on top and cheesecake with fresh strawberries. Trish looked longingly at the Mud Pie but gave it up. The piece was so huge it could have been a whole meal.

As they each took bites from both desserts, Trish brought up her dream from the night before. "It was so strange; all the horses kept running away from me. Even Spitfire. I cried and cried for him to come back but it was like he couldn't."

Marge leaned on her elbows on the table. "Sounds to me like it has something to do with racing. How did you feel?"

"Afraid. Mad. Like crying. I was crying in the dream." Trish nibbled on one of the raspberries. "It was like they were all mad at me."

"Sure." David snorted. " 'Cause you'd quit racing."

"But I haven't quit yet."

"But you might. Who knows. It was just a dream anyway."

"You can pray for an answer to the dream too, you know," Marge said. "Oh, and by the way, I almost forgot. I have something for you." Trish waited while her mother dug in her purse. "Here." Marge handed Trish an envelope.

Trish opened it and drew out a packet of 3x5 cards. The top was in her father's handwriting. She flipped through them, the tears blurring her eyes. Some were in her handwriting. All of them were Bible verses, the verses that had covered her wall. The verses she had thrown in the trash.

"Oh, Mom." She threw her arms around her mother. "How come you're so smart? I felt terrible about throwing them away."

"I knew you would—someday. When I was dumping the trash, I found them. If you didn't want them, I did."

———

That night, kneeling beside her bed, Trish changed her prayer. Up to then it had always been, "God, what do I do?" Now she prayed, "Father, not my will but yours. Whatever you want me to do, that's what I want."

Just before she fell asleep, she was sure she heard Nagger give a deep sigh. Was it approval?

She awoke to butterflies but they calmed down during morning works. She and Firefly trotted around the track like this wasn't a big day, just an ordinary one.

When Trish began her warm-up routine before the race, the butterflies flipped cartwheels along with her hamstring stretches. They fluttered up into her throat when she laid her head on her knees. But they were flying in formation when she stood beside David and Adam in the saddling paddock.

"Riders up," the announcer called over the loud-speaker.

Trish blinked her eyes as David boosted her into the saddle. Firefly snorted and pawed one front hoof. The sights and sounds around them receded like the fog in the morning. Trish looked from David to her mother to Adam. They all seemed to shimmer in a sea of peace, surrounded by a halo of light in the shadowed stalls.

The bugle notes echoed from outside. The parade to

post. Would this be her last one?

Your will, Father, your will.

Her mother's smile said I love you. Words weren't necessary.

"You can do it, Tee." David gripped her knee. He too was saying I love you in the best way he knew how.

"Just do your best." Adam backed the filly up and led her out to the pony rider.

Trish could hear the announcer introducing the horses as they trotted into the sunshine from under the stands. The roar of the crowd set Firefly to dancing.

"You love it, don't ya, girl?" Trish waved to the stands and stroked the filly's arched neck. She felt like laughing out loud. What an incredibly wonderful, beautiful day! A song from Bible Camp ran through her mind: *Rise and shine, and give God the glory, glory* . . . The tune made her want to sing and dance.

The filly did it for her. They entered the starting gate, all seven horses without a slip-up. Trish and Firefly settled for the break.

The gates flew open and they were off. The field bunched together and didn't start stringing out until the first turn. Firefly ran easily with two other horses, Trish letting one set the pace with Firefly hanging to the right and just off the pace. Going down the backstretch, the three ran four lengths in front of the rest of the field.

Trish crooned her love song into the filly's ears as they went into the far turn. Soon it would be time to make their move. The horse behind them pulled even as they came out of the turn. The jockey in front went to the whip.

"Now! Let's go, Firefly." The filly lengthened out. She gained on the front-runner, stride by stride. The horse on her right dropped off. With a furlong to go, they ran neck and neck.

"Come on, girl, you can do it." Trish willed the filly forward. She could see the finish line. "Come on."

Firefly stretched again. Her hooves and heart thundered together. She inched in front. By a nose, by a neck. They won by a length.

"Thank you, Father!" Trish yelled to the heavens, her whip raised in salute.

She pulled the filly down to a gallop, then a lope, and turned back to the front of the grandstands. To the winner's circle.

"You did it, girl. I knew you had it in you." She stroked the filly's neck.

David got to her first. He thumped on her knee, failing miserably at racing decorum. He led them through the fence and over to the raisers.

Marge and Adam met them in the winner's circle. Trish sniffed back her tears until she saw her mother's face, wet with joy.

"Good ride, my dear." Adam looked up at her and nodded. They lined up around Firefly, posed for the official pictures. The camera flashed. Trish leaped to the ground and more cameras flashed. Trish stepped on the scale, all the while her heart singing, *Give God the glory, glory.*

"You sure got your answer," David said as they walked Trish back to the jockey room for her things.

"Yep, that I did."

As she came out, a reporter stopped her. "Got a minute, Trish?"

Trish looked at him in surprise. "Sure, why?"

"This is your first win since the Belmont, right?"

Trish nodded. "I've been following your career," the young man said. "Think we'll head this 'The Comeback Kid.' You've had a hard time and I want you to know I've been rooting for you."

Trish swallowed her state of shock and answered a few more questions.

"Is that right about a possible endorsement for Chrysler?"

"What?" Trish blinked at the question. "Where'd you hear that?"

"I have my sources." His grin said he wouldn't tell her.

"Well, it's news to me."

"Here's my card. When you know more, would you give me a call?"

Trish shrugged. "Sure, I guess."

"Endorsement!" David choked on the word.

"Yeah, right. He's got his wires crossed, that's all. Can we get something to drink. I'm dying."

————

That night in bed, Trish thought back to the winner's circle. It was like she was standing off to the side so she could see everyone there. David held the reins, standing in front of Firefly's shoulder. Adam, Martha, and Carlos stood behind on the raisers. Just in front of the filly's head stood her mother, and behind her shoulder, a man with a smile to dim the noon sun.

She could finally picture her father with the family. And what better place than in the winner's circle?

Monday evening David drove Trish to the College of San Mateo. "Now, I'll be sitting out here praying for you. Tee, you're going to do fine. Just remember to ask for help; pray your way through this."

"But I need a B to get a C out of the class." Trish clamped her lips on her moan. *I've got to pray my way through this.* She squared her shoulders and marched into the classroom.

An hour and a half later she returned to the car, sank into the seat, and closed her eyes.

"Rough?"

"Yeah." Sprinklers sang on the lawn. Trish sniffed. They'd mowed the grass recently. She took in a deep breath. "Davy, my boy, there were only two questions I had no idea about. And only a few I had to guess on. I *think* I did it."

"Mom's waiting at the Finleys'. They think we should go for hot fudge sundaes. What do you think?"

"Yes!" She turned the ignition. "Yes! Yes! Yes!"

That night Trish and Marge sat out on the deck before going to bed. "I am so proud of you," Marge said after letting the night silence steal over them.

"Me, too." Trish looked up at the stars over the eucalyptus trees. "You know what?"

"What?"

"I think I learned something."

"Only one thing?" Marge chuckled. "What is it?"

"I think when things get tough, all you can do is grab God's hand and slog through."

"True, that's the best way."

"And if you slog long enough, you'll come out of the mist . . ." She paused. ". . . and into the sunlight."

"Ah, Tee, you are wise beyond your years."

The breeze set the leaves above them to whispering.

"I have something for you to take to Pastor Mort."

"What?"

"A letter, and the title to the other convertible. He can use the money from it however he wants, but it's to be a memorial to Dad. That okay?"

"Trish, that's more than okay. You truly are your father's daughter."

Trish was sure she heard a chuckling on the breeze.

I'd like to thank all those kids who read my books and beg for more. Writers need readers. We're all in this together. That's part of being in the family of God. Hoorah!